THE BRAZEN PEACOCK

OTHER BOOKS IN THE
H. BEDFORD-JONES UNIFORM
EDITION LIBRARY:

The Brazen Peacock

The Devil's Bosun

Ghost Hills

Invitation to a Crime:
Further Adventures of Denis Burke

Our Far Flung Battle Line

Tyrone of New Orleans

Will o' the Wisp

H . BEDFORD-JONES

THE BRAZEN PEACOCK

H. BEDFORD-JONES

ALTUS PRESS • 2016

© 2016 Altus Press • First Edition—2016

EDITED AND DESIGNED BY
Matthew Moring

PUBLISHING HISTORY
"The Brazen Peacock" originally appeared in the August–October, 1920 issues of *The Blue Book* magazine (Vol. 31, Nos. 4-6).

THANKS TO
Everard P. Digges LaTouche and Gerd Pircher

TABLE OF CONTENTS

CHAPTER I

TO TELL THE WHOLE HISTORY OF ONE MAN REQUIRES
A THOUSAND AND FOURSCORE VOLUMES; BECAUSE NO
MAN'S LIFE IS OF HIMSELF ALONE, AND NO SCRIBE MAY
INDITE THE ENTIRETY THEREOF.—*AL BARANI*.

A SLEETY RAIN was increasing the dusk as the limousine drew up beneath the wide porte-cochère of a stately mansion in Central Park West. The chauffeur whipped open the door. Howard Z. Fraser left the limousine and the cold rain and entered into the luxurious loneliness which he called home.

"Come to the library," he said to Winkler when the latter took his coat and hat.

He passed on through the empty rooms; the massive furnishings and wondrous blends of color—for which he had paid the decorators their thousands—seemed not to appeal to him. He passed on to a room which no decorator had mishandled, the one room in this great mansion which Fraser could rightly call his own, the one room which he loved.

It was a bare room. On the floor was a Kurdish rug, much tattered, reeking of camels and nameless dirt; Fraser had fetched it from the Orient in other years. A battered old desk, an armchair which showed bulging springs, two or three photographs on the walls, a cheap bookcase that sagged beneath the weight of thumbed mining reports, fantastic works of fiction, popular magazines—most amazing surroundings to be chosen, by this wizard of oil, mining and transportation! But Howard Z. Fraser had not chosen these things. He had begun with them, years ago, and now cherished them as old friends from the estate of poverty.

Fraser took a cigaret from the open tantalus, lighted it and sank into the armchair. He tried to smoke, but found no pleasure of the tobacco. While he sat gazing, Winkler brought in a cocktail, because it was the thing to do, though Fraser invariably ignored it.

Winkler was a tall, emaciated man of no apparent emotions. Twenty years as the Fraser's family butler had frozen Winkler into the perfectly proper, placid servant that he was. Yet upon occasion, when addressed as a human being, he could show just the interest one desires in a confidant—no more, no less. *Précis!* There were unplumbed deeps to Winkler, however.

"Winkler," said Fraser abruptly, as the other set down his tray, "do you know how old I am?"

"Yes sir. Forty-eight next December, sir."

"A man of forty-seven isn't good for much, is he?"

"If I may remark, sir, you are young for your age."

"A kindly but abominable lie, Winkler."

FRASER GLANCED again at the mirror. He saw but a faint reflection of the features of his lost son—the son whom he had goaded into fleeing afar. His own hair was prematurely gray. His face was a bit heavy, very aggressive, the mouth clenched and the eyes masterful, the hawk-nose thin and biting: the face of one who had worked hard, suffered much, learned to repress self.

One sensed here a man of indomitable force and action, a man of strong, heady impulse eased by the cooler reason of age, a man given not to ethics but to results—a materialist whose greatest sin was defeat, whose greatest crime was failure. Such indeed was Howard Z. Fraser, whose untold wealth and com-

mercial interests extended everywhere, into every country, and whose only moral code was to live clean and to fight like hell.

"A lie, Winkler," he repeated. "I look nearly sixty. I wish to ask you something!"

"Yes sir."

"Do you remember a certain rainy night like this, over two years ago; and do you recall what transpired in this room then?"

The calm, undistinguished features of Winkler became momentarily ruffled, as a calm pool of water is ruffled by the leap of a fish.

"Yes sir."

"You were present during that interview, Winkler. It was the last time I saw Bob. Do you recall the conversation between Bob and me?"

"I do, sir."

Fraser seemed about to say something, then checked himself. He looked again at the mirror. His lips slowly clenched.

Like other men of affairs, he had gone to Washington at a dollar a year. Now he was home once more in New York; but he was not happy; work could not brighten the winter of his discontent. He was a bitterly hard man; he had built up large things, and he was without scruples. In his younger days he had spent some time in the Orient, laying there the foundations upon which had been erected his imposing edifice of wealth and power. The Orient, however, had not affected the harsh crudity of his nature. He was an extremist, and he had been a cynic; but during the past two years he had been whelmed under a tide of loneliness. Now, on trying to return to his own business, he had found it vain. So he had tried to find again the son who was lost; and he had failed.

It was evening in New York, but upon the other side of the world it was morning. Fraser felt a certain abominable reek penetrating to his thin nostrils; he glanced down at the tattered and dirty old Kurdish rug. He felt himself queerly drawn to that other side of the world where his son had vanished; he felt drawn by an attraction deeper than himself, an attraction which he could not resist. Perhaps there was something of mental telepathy in this attraction. Across the world, at this moment, another man had Fraser heavily in mind; destiny moves strangely in these matters.

SUDDENLY FRASER looked up at the motionless servant. His face hardened into iron.

"Winkler, if you recall that conversation, kindly repeat it word for word."

Again the calm countenance became ruffled. "If you please, sir—"

"Repeat it!" snapped Fraser, stirring uneasily. "Cut out the pose, and do as I say!"

Winkler drew a deep breath. "Well, sir, Mr. Robert had been drinking, and you had been working very hard indeed. You used harsh words, sir. Mr. Robert admitted that they were justified. You became angry, and mentioned your intention of cutting him adrift, and he—er—"

"Go on," said Fraser in a dead voice, as Winkler paused.

"He told you to go to hell with your money, sir, that he wanted none of it. And then, sir, you—you flared up and called him—"

Winkler's voice fell away, but Fraser repeated his curt command.

"Go on."

Obeying the order, Winkler repeated what Fraser had called his son. It was not a nice term. It was not what a gentleman would have said. It was what a rough man would call his own son only in the bitter heat of passion—not meaning the words, but deeming his son a wastrel and a drunken blackguard, useless and inefficient.

"Well?" prompted Fraser, his voice still cold and dead. "Then what?"

"Mr. Robert struck you, sir, and left the house."

"Struck me?" Fraser uttered a cackle of bitter laughter. "Knocked hell out of me, you mean! And right! If he hadn't done it, he'd have been worse than yellow. I suppose, Winkler, you slipped him some money before he left?"

The expressionless face of Winkler hardened into surprisingly icy lines.

"If I may say so, sir, that is none of your business."

"Ah!" Fraser glanced up at him suddenly, keenly, his blue eyes hard as stone. "Ah! Your impassivity has been pierced, eh? Good! Now, then, Winkler, speak up! You have theories; I haven't known you twenty years for nothing! Speak up and tell me exactly how this affair with Bob struck you; tell me just where I went astray with him."

Winkler met the flinty blue eyes with an even flintier gaze.

"I would rather, sir, that you did not insist."

"I do insist," said Fraser acidly. "I want your frank opinion— Heaven knows I should have asked for it long ago!"

Winkler permitted himself a shrug of resignation.

"Very well," he answered in a changed voice. "My opinion is that Mr. Robert did exactly the right thing when he knocked you across that desk. For years, ever since the death of Mrs. Fraser, Mr. Robert was allowed to do as he wished. You were always too busy to give him any attention except when he got into trouble and you were forced to remember his existence. You considered your duty done when you gave him money to spend.

"I am not a family man myself, sir, but I could tell that this state of things would end up in disaster. It was your own fault, sir—your fault entirely. Of course, in his words to you on that evening, one must admit that Mr. Robert spoke most injudiciously. That is all. I do not think that you can complain of my services, sir. If you will write me a brief character, I shall have my things packed immediately."

He turned to leave the room. Fraser's voice halted him.

"Wait! You mean that you are leaving me?"

"I hardly fancy that you would care to have me stay, sir, after—"

"Winkler, I'm an old fool; that's the truth." Fraser slumped down a little in his chair. "You sha'n't leave. In fact, I'll need you during the next few months, and Bob will need you also. I've not had a word from him since he left here. However, I presume he wrote you?"

"He did, sir."

"Then you may know that he joined the British army, was sent to Mesopotamia, has been there ever since, and has become an officer on the Intelligence staff."

"Yes sir." Winkler waited, imperturbable.

"I sent him a cable last week, Winkler—the first word I've addressed to him since that night in this room. I apologized for what had happened and requested him to come home at once. A reply came today—but not from Bob. It came from his former commanding officer!"

"Former?" Winkler licked his lips suddenly. "You—you don't mean—"

Fraser threw out his hands in a gesture of helplessness.

"No, not dead, thank God! But lost, Winkler—lost! He—"

"Where?" said Winkler thickly. "Where was this?"

"Bagdad. After the armistice he asked for discharge and got it. They don't know where he is—somewhere up in the hills exploring a ruin. There were two of them, Bob and some fool Englishman—an archaeologist. They went off together and vanished. Nobody has time to search, I suppose."

"Your agents in Palestine and Persia—"

"Everything is shot to pieces over there." Fraser shook his head. "I've got to start an entirely new organization—and handle it in person. There are big pickings to be had in that country, and I mean to get in on them—"

"Damn!" said Winkler, blinking suddenly. "Damn your pickings! Have you no heart? Have you no idea except *money*—"

Fraser snarled, wolflike—bared his fangs, cursing.

"Don't you know me, you fool?" he finished. "I'm going after the boy."

"To that country? Yourself?"

"Think I'm too damned old and useless, do you? Think I'm worked out, eh? You've got another think coming. I'm going, and I intend to find my boy! If he's come to grief, Lord help the man that did it! I've got friends there still, maybe. If old Tahir Beg is still alive, he'll ride through all hell with me for friendship; twenty years ago we rode and did our killing together—I hope he's still living.

"I've made myself what I am. I don't claim to be any high-falutin' nobility or blueblood. I'm an American! I know I'm rough—I was made rough, and it was rough work put me where I am today.... About Bob, now; I was wrong in the old days, wrong in trying to handle him roughly that night. He should have had enough sense to know that a man does not mean a cuss-word literally. Well, no matter! I'm going over there, and you're going with me."

Winkler stood aghast, then suddenly remembered his position.

"If I may say so, sir," he suggested with some agitation, "it's hardly feasible! For one thing, transportation—"

Fraser named his yacht. "The *Geraldine* is out of the Government service. She's making ready for the run now. We leave in three days—go direct to Bagdad."

"But, sir, the British government—"

"Has my credentials on the way from Washington. I've handled things by wire today." Fraser smiled grimly. "A little pep left in the old man, eh?"

"Yes sir. But among the heathen, sir—"

"Damn the heathen, and you too! Haven't I been there before, you blithering idiot? Didn't I spend two years in Persia and Kurdistan looking for oil—and finding it? Haven't I friends there among the heathen? I can pick up the language again in a few weeks—used to know it like a book. You go and pack up."

"Yes sir." Winkler hesitated. "Just the two of us, sir?"

"Yes. We leave the yacht at Bagdad, if we can get up the river, and go by rail to Samara, where we'll meet Bob's commander. We'll get full information there, then go after the boy. Want to back out, do you?"

"Not I, sir." Winkler discreetly closed the library door before allowing himself to grin widely.

Fraser rose to his feet when he was alone and took a book from the mantel. One observed now that his shoulders were remarkably square; the sense of his virility was much increased by this square width, and by the powerful set of his head. From the book he took a small photograph. One might have fancied that his hard blue eyes grew suspiciously moist as he gazed at the picture. It was the picture of a boy.

ON THE evening these things happened in New York, it was morning upon the other side the world. Here, in a very different setting and atmosphere, another man was also talking of Bob Fraser—a man fully as remarkable in his own sphere as was Howard Z. Fraser in the sphere of commerce. This man was named Tahir Beg.

Tahir Beg, although he lived and held rule among the Hamavand Kurds, was by birth a scion of the proudest and wildest of all the tribes of the Persian borderland—the Aormani, who acknowledge the rule of no suzerain, and who claim descent from Rustam, the titular hero of Persia.

Except for his five cartridge-belts, his rifle and pistols, his gayly embroidered dress and silk turban, Tahir Beg might have posed for a Norse Viking. No sign of gray had touched his yellow hair, although he had seen fifty winters. In his rocklike, ruggedly handsome features blazed eyes of an icy, piercing gray, now cruel with unrestrained passion, now tender beyond belief.

The long yellow mustache that hung six inches below his lips did not hide the steely mouth and massive chin, the long, powerful jaw. Tahir Beg stood six feet four in his boots, and in all his world there was but one person who could meet his anger without quailing. To this person he was now talking.

"Little jewel of the hills," he said gently, "word has come that an Englishman lies ill at Erbil. The name is the name of a friend of my youth, although there is faint chance that the two men are the same, for Englishmen and Americans all have names that sound alike. Still, I am going to protect this dying man because of a certain ancient friendship. What shall I bring you from Erbil, little jewel?"

The girl before him smiled into his eyes. She answered him in Persian, not in Kurdish.

"Is it not true, my father, that the Englishmen have driven the Turks out of all the land? Then bring me this Englishman, if he is not dead. I want to see one of them!"

Tahir Beg laughed hugely at this. None the less in his piercing gray eyes sat a strange wonder and uneasiness, as though some inner thing troubled him after many years.

"By the lord of the faithful!" He swore, like a true Shi'a, by Ali. "An Englishman rather than silks or jewels? So be it. If this man, Agha Fraser, should by any chance be my ancient friend, then I shall bring him; Englishmen and Americans are the same breed. Mind you, he was the only man who could ever best me at fighting or wrestling! Aie, but he was wild in his rage!"

A swift merriment leaped to the girl's face.

"Oh!" she cried. "Then bring him, bring him, and let him fight you!"

Tahir Beg roared with laughter, and rightly. Many a man had courted this daughter of his; yet her heart had inclined to none; and among the Kurds, the people of freedom, there is great liberty as regards marriage. Also Tahir Beg had announced that no man might woo the daughter unless man enough to fight the father and beat him—a thing which no man yet had done. Thus, Tahir Beg preserved to himself the one thing he loved in the world. The remainder of his family were long since dead, destroyed by the Turks.

SO TAHIR BEG departed northward toward Erbil, swinging up the valley on his fine horse, with another fine horse trailing behind. He rode alone, as he was ever wont to ride; Tahir Beg feared neither brigand nor feudist foe. He might be gone a week or a month, but he was never known to come home poorer than when he had departed. Behind him, in the valley nestling under the snowy mountains, she whom all men knew as the daughter of Tahir Beg held his house immaculate against his return, and bore herself with the proud freedom of the Kurdish woman. But this girl was not a woman of the Kurds; nor was she any daughter of Tahir Beg—although this was known only to Tahir Beg and one other.

To the south of the Hamavand country, and roughly dividing their territory from that ruled by the Jaf tribes, lay Sulaimanieh, a city ruled and ruined by a family of Shaiks or religious leaders. This was a family strong in crime, in ruthless and cruel power, in long and bloody association with the Turk. Young Shaik Nuri, newly come to rule, was even then departing for Samara in order to interview the British authorities and make arrangements that would sustain him in power under the new lords of the land.

Now, Samara lay in the Tigris valley, over the Kara Dagh mountains to the southwest; but Shaik Nuri rode to the north. He did this because he had business in Erbil, where lived his uncle Kadir. A wily old fox was Kadir, who had lived long among the Turks and who knew the outside world very well. Kadir had too many blood-feuds on his hands to venture south into Kurdish territory, for in his day Kadir had led many Turkish troops to massacre and rapine among the mountains. So the old fox stayed in Erbil.

Shaik Nuri desired to consult Kadir and learn of the fox's wisdom before seeing the British; he had been somewhat concerned in the Armenian massacres, and was not certain what lies to tell. Thus it happened that Shaik Nuri summoned his horsemen and rode north from the gasping city which the bloody misrule of his house had transformed from a great trading center into a ruined town shunned by all travelers.

Shaik Nuri had never heard of Tahir Beg, although the latter might have heard of him. He bore letters to the Hamavand chiefs, and was given safe-conduct through their country. Halting for a meal near the stead of Tahir Beg, he chanced to see the chieftain's daughter; and seeing her, he was amazed. His men dutifully made inquiries for him, and Shaik Nuri realized at once that here was a prize well worth the winning.

He said nothing, as was his fashion, and rode on toward Erbil with the image of Tahir Beg's daughter breeding maggots in his evil brain. Why not send his uncle Kadir down to Samara to parley with the British? Then he himself could be free to cast his nets! And already Shaik Nuri had a shrewd suspicion as to what net he would cast for that girl.

Marry her he could not, for already he had the lawful number of wives, and the men of Sulaimanieh are famed for their rabid fanaticism in the law of Islam. However, these things did not worry Shaik Nuri. He was a young man, of unbridled passion, and he gave small heed to affairs of religion. Looking back at the riders who followed him, he saw among them more than one man wearing a shirt close-buttoned about his neck—which is not Kurdish fashion; and seeing them, Shaik Nuri laughed softly to himself. These men had come out of Persia to him, and they were worshipers of Satan; and Shaik Nuri had made alliance with their chief. So Shaik Nuri saw what manner of net he would use when he returned home, and smiled again.

Having woven thus the tangled skein of men's lives, the fates laid it aside for the deeds of men to finish.

CHAPTER II

NONE OF US IS ALLOWED TO UTTER HIS NAME, NOR
ANYTHING THAT RESEMBLES IT.—*THE BLACK BOOK.*

"**P**OOR OLD Harrowgate!" muttered Bob Fraser. He stared about the bare, whitewashed little room with its barred window. "Poor old Harrowgate!"

An hour previously Harrowgate had been buried. Now Bob Fraser, sitting in the little room in the upper story of the Erbil caravanserai, considered his position and found it anything but pleasant.

Harrowgate, an archaeologist of some eminence, had been in the intelligence section of the "Mespot" expeditionary force. With peace, the two friends had left the army, had come up north to Erbil. It was Harrowgate's dream, this coming to Erbil. Fraser had accompanied him out of friendship, curiosity, vivid interest.

Beneath the town of Erbil was a mountain, a monstrous mound rising from the Galley. In that mound lay buried the temples of Ishtar, for a thousand years the greatest shrine of the ancient world—during two thousand years more, lost in ruins. Harrowgate dreamed of digging into that great mound. Then, at the very outset, fever smote the dreamer; and now he was dead and gone, buried in the desolate cemetery outside town. This place was the ancient Arbela, where Alexander had

stepped to the world's throne. Bob Fraser reflected upon the
fact with bitter irony, applying it to his own position.

The caravanserai was decent and comfortable. Fraser had a
little money, a good knowledge of Kurdish and Persian, unlim-
ited ambition and no prospects. As he sat there sucking at his
pipe, he looked very unlike the dissipated young scamp who
had left New York years previously. Sun and desert had bitten
him to a blackish red, through which pierced the startling clear-
ness of his blue eyes. His hair was sun-bleached to a tow-color.
His face, perched above abnormally wide shoulders, was not
handsome. It was marked by a large, thin-curved nose, a straight,
hard mouth, and harshly bitter lines. It was the face of one who
had worked hard, suffered much and learned self-repression.
Bob Fraser had been forgetting how to smile. He looked like
a man of thirty instead of twenty-four. Yet in his face was a
wealth of character.

"Cursed if I know what to do!" he reflected gloomily, refilling
his pipe. "I've money enough to get out of the country—if I
want to go. But what then? Day labor? Not if I can help it. Day
labor in the tropics is plain hell."

A LOUD and arrogant knocking at the door interrupted his
cogitations. "Come in!" called Fraser in Kurdish. The door
opened to admit Tahir Beg.

"*Salamun 'alaikum!*" proclaimed the chieftain sonorously,
twirling his mustaches.

"*Alaikum as salam*—and with you, peace!" Fraser rose. He
wondered what this splendid ruffian wanted with him, and why
the gray eyes devoured him with such fierce intensity. Some
new attempt at graft or robbery, perhaps.

Tahir Beg swaggered into the room, slammed the door
behind him with a fine disdain for its hinges, and kept his gaze
fastened upon Fraser.

"*Bi haqq i 'amiru'l mu'minin!*" he ejaculated in Persian. "Know
you the tongue of Shiraz? And from what part of Frangistan
come you?"

Fraser answered in the same tongue, for he had become used to this direct curiosity in his personal affairs, which was a custom of the land.

"I do not come from Frangistan, but from a farther land, from America."

"By the right of the lord of the faithful!" exclaimed Tahir Beg again, delight leaping into his eyes. "Sixteen years ago there was a man from America, a man named Fraser. I heard that one named Agha Farizur lay here dying, and I came to see. Now I find that the report carried the name amiss; it was another man who lay ill, and who is now dead. Yet you are here, and it is evident that you are your father's son! Your father was my friend."

"Ah!" Bob Fraser was startled, incredulous. "You knew my father?"

Although he was aware that during his own childhood his father had been in this land, he had not expected any such recognition as this. Indeed, his father had seldom spoken of the time spent in Persia. It was a subject on which the lips of Howard Z. Fraser seemed closed.

"Somewhat—somewhat!" The Kurd laughed fiercely. "I am Gholam Ali Tahir Beg Aorami. Your father was my friend and comrade, and we fought stirrup to stirrup; therefore you are my friend. If it please you to ride home with me, Allah will honor my house greatly."

Tahir Beg shook hands and seated himself. Fraser produced a samovar and provisions, and brewed tea; his guest gladly laid aside the Kurdish cigarets of powdered tobacco in favor of the English brand offered him, and fell to talking.

"Years ago," reflected Tahir Beg, covertly studying his host, "this was a proper land, with Turks and Persians and Russians fighting each other. Today the good old times are gone. The English rule in the valleys, or will rule shortly; there will be no more of the grand riding and fighting I had with your father! However," he added resignedly, "one can always ride into Persia if nothing else offers, and in the hills the name of Englishman is unknown. There is still mercy in Allah's dispensation—God, the Compassionate, the Indivisible! Swords are still sharp in the hills. We may slay those who worship Shaitan."

FRASER SHOOK his head. He had poured tea, and he was now repaying the scrutiny of Tahir Beg with a scrutiny equally close and keen.

"I seek no fighting, Tahir Beg; I've had my fill of that, the past two years. So you are living among the Hamavands, eh? A fighting people, from what I hear; a few years ago their warriors defied the whole Turkish army."

"I had some hand in that myself." Tahir Beg complacently stroked his long yellow mustache. "The Turks are fools and cowards; I am glad that the English have taken over the rule! You people and the English are all one. I remember when your father rode into the hills with me, and we carried off the girls from Sufiz—ah, he was a fighter, your father! And something of a devil, eh? We were young in those days, and the world was good."

"You do not look so old," said Fraser.

"Old? By Allah, thirty is too old after one passes it! Still," added the chieftain, "I think there are few men who can stand before me. Your father was one of them. You, by your shoulders, might be another. We must try—"

A knock sounded at the door. Fraser called to enter; the door opened to admit a boy of the town, who thrust at Fraser a small brass object.

"The charge is two piasters, *agha*," he mumbled in the villainous local dialect, compounded of Turkish and Kurdish.

Fraser angrily protested the charge. The boy whiningly argued the matter, being content in the end to depart with half the amount demanded. As the boy turned from the door, Fraser saw him exchange a word with a dark-faced Kurd lingering in the corridor. Fraser stepped into the doorway. The Kurd came up to him with an insolent swagger.

"Listen to me, infidel!" said the Kurd. "Do you understand my tongue?"

"Perfectly," said Fraser, holding the brass object in his hand. "What do you want?"

"That brazen peacock." The Kurd thrust forward his hand as if to snatch the thing, but Fraser quietly put the object into his pocket, whereat the man cursed. "Hear and obey, infidel dog! My master is Shaik Nuri, whose word is law in the hills! He saw this brazen bird as it was being fetched to you; it is one which was stolen from him last week on the road, and he bade me bring it to him again. So hand it here—"

Fraser caught the Kurd's shoulder, whirled the insolent one around, and kicked him down the corridor.

"You and your master lie—take back this message," he said, and with a last kick sent the messenger rolling down the stairway.

He returned to the room, to find Tahir Beg standing at the door, laughing heartily.

"By the lord of the faithful, that was your father's way!" chuckled the chieftain, and closed the door again when Fraser had entered. "This dog from Sulaimanieh learned a good lesson—there is no devil in all the land like Shaik Nuri, young though he be in years! And what was it that he so desired, brother?"

"This." Fraser drew the brazen object from his pocket. "I picked it up in Samara, and it was so corroded that when we came here, I left it with a merchant in the street of the brass workers to have it cleaned and polished. What it is I know not—some relic of antiquity, eh?"

TAHIR BEG examined the thing with interest. It was a conventionalized bird shape, and had once been elegantly chased, but the lines were now nearly effaced. Beneath it was a threaded projection, denoting that it was a part of some ornament or larger object. Obviously it was of great age.

"It is strange to me," said Tahir Beg, frowning, "and yet it has the look of Persian work. Somewhere I have seen something like it, but so many years ago that the memory has gone from me. Well! Since Shaik Nuri wants the thing, it has some value; keep it! Will you ride home with me? If so, let us be gone from this accursed city. This crowded abode of men stifles my lungs, and these insolent folk tempt me to bloodshed each moment!"

Fraser had already made his decision.

"Gladly," he assented. "In ten minutes I shall be ready. This Shaik Nuri seems to have little knowledge of men, to send so insolent a message to me! You know him?"

"I know of him," said Tahir Beg, watching Fraser while the latter packed into his saddlebags what he wished to take. "And no man knows good of him. He and his family have devastated a rich city, know no law save their own will, and are allied with all the rogues and thieves in the land. In these days of upheaval the Shaiks—for so the family and tribe are called— may do as they like with impunity. They were greatly concerned in the massacres of the Armenian folk during the war; they brought home much booty, filled their harems with young girls and learned many evil things."

"You were not concerned in those massacres, then?" said Fraser, pausing.

"I?" Tahir Beg puffed out his cheeks, and his eyes began to blaze. "Am I a butcher of sheep or a free man of the hills? By the lord of the faithful! It is not our way to ally ourselves with those Turcoman Kurds of the north, who serve the Turks! Bah!"

Save for the incident with the insolent visitor, Fraser might not have bothered to carry the brazen bird with him, since its weight was no trifle; for many days he had forgotten its very possession. However, he decided to take his companion's advice and so thrust the brass into a corner of his bags. After all, it might have some tangible value.

"Ready!" he exclaimed. "Your horse is here?"

"Mine, and a spare one for you."

"I have two—my own and that of my dead friend."

"So much the better, by Allah! We may have need of spare mounts. Let us go!"

Tahir Beg led the way from the corridor to the stairway that passed into the central courtyard of the inn, and Fraser, carrying his saddle-bags, followed. He had that morning sent off Harrowgate's few effects to Samara, and there was nothing to detain him here.

Leaving Tahir Beg to get the horses, Fraser sought the innkeeper and settled his score, arranging to leave some of his effects until his return. The host, a scowling fellow of the local Baban breed, gave him a keen glance.

"Have a care what road you follow, *agha*," he muttered into his beard. "Within the last few minutes there has been swift and bitter talk concerning you."

"Eh?" Fraser eyed him in surprise. "What mean you?"

"If I knew more, I might tell more," and the other shrugged. "There are more strangers here today than devils in hell, and I know little. May God requite your generosity and lighten the pains of hell for the dead infidel who was your friend! He was a good man."

FROWNING A little, Fraser turned to the courtyard, which was filled with a motley throng of travelers, beggars, merchants and peddlers. As he made his way toward Tahir Beg, he did not wonder that the warning of his host had been vague; the place was a babel of tongues and dialects. The warning itself might well have been some ruse to provoke generosity.

As Fraser thought thus, he felt a hand clutch at his elbow and turned swiftly. A young man, handsomely dressed, was saluting him; speaking in Persian, he said smilingly:

"I am Nuri al Hallaj, Shaik of Sulaimanieh. I wish to ask your pardon for the disgraceful conduct of my man, and to crave a moment's speech with you."

Fraser was no little astonished at this speech, for Shaik Nuri was clearly not the type to offer apologies freely. He was a young man, handsome in a wild and ferocious manner; sensuality and cruelty were stamped in his whole countenance.

About the two men had gathered others; these, from their weapons and costumes, were southern Kurds, followers of the young chief. Fraser gathered from their looks that the bad Persian spoken by their master was not intelligible to them, for among the southern Kurds the tongue is almost unknown.

"I accept your courtesy, Shaik Nuri," answered Fraser in the same tongue, "and thank you for it. As for speech, however, I am leaving here immediately in some haste. If you have anything to say, let it be said here."

The dark eyes of the Shaik flashed for an instant, as though lighted by some inner fury at this brusque response; but still the red and sensual lips maintained their friendly smile.

"Very well." Nuri dropped into Kurdish. "It is of no great importance, perhaps. I am traveling toward the south, and learning that you were of the army of Frangistan, I thought that you might travel in my company and tell me of that army."

"I am not going thither," said Fraser shortly. "I am leaving here with a friend, whose road goes south and east."

Once more he caught that wild flash in the eyes of the young chieftain.

"Allah alone disposeth the ways of men!" was the answer. "It may be that I shall send my uncle Kadir to Samara to see these chiefs of Frangistan and make covenant with them. Would such a thing offend them, or must I go myself?"

"If your uncle bears letters giving him authority to speak for you," said Fraser, "no more is necessary. In return, kindly tell me the value of that brass bird, and why your man was so eager to obtain it."

The dark features of the young Shaik flushed at this question. One or two of these standing around gave Fraser fierce looks.

"By the prophet, the fool misunderstood my words!" Nuri broke into a laugh. "I pray you, pardon the error. If you come to Sulaimanieh, I shall be honored to have you as my guest."

FRASER EXPRESSED his thanks and took his departure. As he joined Tahir Beg, he caught a disjointed fragment of speech from one of Shaik Nuri's men, in which occurred the Arabic words *"ma al kabir"* or "great water"—a somewhat roundabout term which Fraser had sometimes heard applied to the Tigris or Euphrates. He thought nothing of it at this moment, since many Arabic words were flying in the air around him.

Tahir Beg grunted some comment on Shaik Nuri, but devoted himself entirely to clearing a way out of the crowded courtyard. After some difficulty this was accomplished. The two men rode through town and descended the winding road which led into the valley below the great mound. Tahir Beg rode in silence, examining the outspread country below them with fierce eyes and pulling at his long mustaches.

Once clear of the town, Fraser recounted his passage with the young chief.

"He lied like a Syrian," he concluded bluntly, "and except for provoking trouble, I should have told him so. His apology was said in Persian that his men might not understand it, and the fact angered me."

Tahir Beg nodded frowningly, but for a moment made no answer. He seemed to be pondering some subject, and paid no heed when Fraser repeated the warning of the innkeeper. Of a sudden he uttered a sharp ejaculation and flung up his head.

"Ah! Those men knew of me, and they knew much! I heard them asking about me. Plainly, they passed through the Hamavand country on their way north. Well, let that go; Allah knows that I have no desire to mingle with them or have aught to do with them!

"Listen, my brother! Just as you joined me, after your speech with that dog, one of his men spoke of the river—"

"I heard him," interjected Fraser. The chieftain turned upon him a look pregnant with unuttered things. The gray eyes were piercing and alight with inner fire.

"Ah! How would you or I speak of the river? What word would we use?"

"The most natural word," answered Fraser, "would be *shatt*."

"By Allah, yes!" cried Tahir Beg, slapping his thigh a resounding thwack. "And the speaker wore, under his cloak, a shirt that came close up around his neck! Know you what that means?"

Fraser shook his head. It was evident that some violent excitement had gripped his companion, and he was vaguely disturbed by the fact. He felt that in Tahir Beg resided a wildly boyish spirit—a madcap lust after trouble and peril.

"You have heard of the Yezidis?" demanded the Kurd. "The infidels who worship Shaitan?"

"Vaguely. Devil-worshipers—"

"Aye!" Tahir Beg nodded emphatically. "They not only worship him, but they greatly venerate his name. They will never use a word like *shatt* which even resembles it in sound. By the lord of the faithful! That speaker was one of them!

"They were broken by the Turk; many of them inhabit the mountains south of Aoraman, and I have heard that they have a new chieftain called Uthman al Hudr, who has gathered them about him in the Penjivan district. By Allah, I believe that Shaik Nuri has allied himself with this Al Hudr! They worship the symbol of the devil, a brazen peacock; always they refer to Shaitan by the name of Melek Taus, or King Peacock—"

"What!" Fraser started. "You mean that the—"

"Aye, the brazen bird, brother!" Tahir Beg bellowed out the words exultantly, furiously, gayly. "By the right of the lord of the faithful, it is one of their lost gods,—lost twenty years ago when the Turk swept them,—one of the seven images they have worshiped since the days of King Solomon, who wrought them from brass. Seven there were, and five were stolen by the Turks; and this is one of the five! And now it is known that you have it! Shaik Nuri, may Ali curse him, wanted it because he is allied with these idolaters! Praise be to God, there will be some excitement to brighten our days!"

Fraser was not so thankful. It did not seem to him very probable that the brazen bird in his saddlebags would cause much stir. What abode most in his mind was that Shaik Nuri had been instrumental in the Armenian massacres. It was this, perhaps, which had raised within him a detestation for that young chieftain.

So the two men rode up the valley toward the brave hills of Kurdistan.

CHAPTER III

ONE WHO CURES THE
HURT OF SCORPIONS

A S T H E two rode down the wide valley, they were saluted
with much respect by all upon the road. Not only was
Bob Fraser's uniform greeted hereabouts with awe, but the rich
garb of Tahir Beg marked him as a chieftain. Under his camel
hair *abba* was visible a superb garment of crimson velvet adorned
with gold frogs, and instead of the usual Kurdish cap he wore
a fine cashmere shawl taken in some Persian raid. The trappings
of his horses were equally handsome.

They rode steadily through the day, and in the afternoon
passed the gates of Altun Keupri and through the city; instead
of keeping to the stony highway, Tahir Beg now turned off
abruptly into the hill roads. He had no fear of wandering Kurds,
and wished to avoid the town of Kirkuk.

They were out of the plain now, and entering upon rolling
hills. Far to the east rose billow after billow of mountains cul-
minating in the high snow-peaks of the Zagros ranges, on
Persian soil, now reddened by the descending sun. There lay
Kurdistan outspread before them—the land of the southern
Kurds, mountaineers, free folk through the ages, as are all men
of the highlands. More than one Turkish army had come to
sore grief in those hills: and those deep valleys sheltered a people
that bowed the knee to no conqueror.

As Tahir Beg rode, as he drew out of the dreary hot plain
toward the cool keenness of the mountains, he broke into wild
bursts of song. He was singing, thus, when they rode down into

a little valley where a brook wound between willow trees, and where beside a clump of darker fig-trees stood a small house. Tahir Beg drew rein and studied the place.

"Ah!" he exclaimed. "The house should be empty, but there is a traveler ahead of us. Forward, brother!"

In the doorway of the house, as they rode up, they perceived an old man standing and watching them. His dress was Kurdish, but his headgear, by which the various Kurd tribes are known, was a mere skull-cap bound about with a white kerchief; it told nothing. His long beard was grizzled and matted with dirt, and in a much-scarred face there was set one living eye of a glowing topaz hue. The other eye was gone in a hideous red weal.

As the two dismounted, this old man uttered a tremulous "*Salam aleikum!*" and was obviously relieved when they replied in kind; he gave them the courtesy of a *"marhaba,"* dabbing at his forehead in the complimentary gesture of respect.

"Thanks be unto Allah that you are honest men!" he said in Kurdish. "I am a poor wanderer; yet I have fear of thieves. If you wish to spend the night in this place, it is as much yours as mine; and if I had one of your fine horses, I would travel on with you tomorrow."

"Allah loves charity," quoth Tahir Beg callously, "but charity may be stretched too far. If you have walked here, then continue—and may Allah be more gracious to you than I! Who are you?"

"I am Ra'sul Majid, and I am going home after ten years of wanderings."

"Whither go you, then?"

"*B'il 'Ajam.*"

"To Persia!" broke in Fraser. "Then you speak Persian?"

"By the curse of the false caliphs!" cried the old man joyfully. "Truly is it said that a word of Persian in a strange land is better than a drink of water in the desert! Enter, my brethren! Enter and enjoy hospitality! *Wah!* To think that I should have heard Persian in the mouth of an Englishman, in the land of

the Kurds! I have seen many wonders; yet this is greater than
the rest."

DISPOSING THE horses under the trees, they brought
in the saddlebags and joined the old Ra'sul Majid. The deserted house boasted a single room, and the old man boasted
little in the way of baggage except dirt. He had, however, a skin
of *du*,—the common Kurdish food, consisting of curds and
whey watered to a minky thinness,—and this he opened gladly.
Fraser added to it bread from their own store, Tahir Beg fetched
figs from the trees near by, and the three settled down to a
sumptuous repast.

Ra'sul Majid talked fluently. He had come, he said, from a
valley in the Persian hills, and had wandered over all the world,
even as far as Saloniki on the east and Samarkand on the west;
his profession was that of a healer of scorpion-stings, and he
sold an oil extracted from the black scorpion, which cured such
hurts.

"Now, since you are an Englishman," he said, addressing
Fraser particularly, "I do not mind saying that in these years I
have put together some little money, and I am taking it home
to Persian Kurdistan. Let us all three go together, since it is
evident that you are men of distinction. You say, Agha Fraser,
that you are no longer in the English army but have served your
time. Then, in the name of Allah, let us join forces. In these
days there are rich pickings to be had among the hills, and you
be worthy brethren. I think that I can gather some few men,
and what is more to the point, I had the luck to learn a great
secret in Kabulistan—a secret that will make us all rich!"

"The secret of what?" said Tahir Beg with a laugh. "Of making
gold from stones?"

The blazing yellow eye of Ra'sul Majid flashed redly in the
light of their small fire. He regarded Tahir Beg for a moment,
then drew back his lips.

"Nay," answered he, "but the secret of putting two drops of
liquid into springs of water, so that all the camels drinking

thereof will lie down and seem to die. When the caravan folks have gone, then I come and give those camels to drink—and lo, they live again and are mine!

"It is well known that Kurds and the Arab camel-men are great enemies; therefore we shall prosper hugely, for the Kurds will be our friends. You twain will gather certain of the Persians to us, and I will answer for certain others. Thus in a month's time we shall have no lack of men at our back, eh? By Allah—"

"By the right of the lord of the faithful!" swore Tahir Beg angrily, "I think that you are a rogue of rogues! And a liar to boot, and an infidel doomed unto hell!"

With a sudden, swift agility, the great Kurd arose. He had caught up a stick in his hand, and now as he rose, he circled that stick about the seated figure of Ra'sul Majid, so that upon the earthen floor of the hut was traced a circle.

Bob Fraser sat back astonished.

THE OLD man was motionless, yet his one eye flared with a mad fury, and for an instant his fingers fumbled at the knife in his belt. He seemed gripped by some impotent whirlwind of anger that brought froth to his lips, while Tahir Beg, placing his hands on his hips, glared down at him with an exultant grin.

"Ha!" cried the Kurd. "Come out of the circle if you can, accursed one! *Na'lat Shaitan!* Accursed be Satan, and all them that worship him! Were you not an old man, and had you not broken bread with me, I would put this knife into your throat for that you dared pretend to be one of the Muslim!"

Now Ra'sul Majid's unlovely countenance broke into a spasm of angry terror.

"Dog that you are!" he cried out. "Break the circle so that I may lie at rest for the night!"

Fraser leaned forward, amazed.

"Break it!" he repeated. "Why, what holds you? There—"

"Peace, brother!" commanded Tahir Beg with a roar of laughter. "Look at him, devil-worshiper that he is! Not one of them but is riddled with superstition—aye, brigands and thieves and worse though they may be, here is one way to encompass them! Now give me that brass bird of yours—"

Diving at the saddle-bags, Tahir Beg brought forth the brazen peacock and set it before the old man, from whom burst a stupefied cry at sight of it.

"Melek Taus! The sacred bearer of the seven candles—"

"Aye, King Peacock!" mocked Tahir Beg. "There is your god, devil-worshiper! There is your god, and here are we, and there are you—unutterable dog that you are, who would dare propose such deviltry to Tahir Beg the Aorami! Now sit there through the night and pray to Shaitan; and if you come into the Hama-vand country, I swear by the holy Ali that I will seat you upon a pointed stake and make you tread air until the stake eats at your evil heart! Come, brother, out of this place of abomination! To think that we ate with this spawn of hell—faugh!"

Leaving the brazen peacock where it was, Tahir Beg caught up the saddle-bags and left the place. Fraser followed, to find him at the brook making the ablutions of his faith.

"Nay, he will be there in the morning, fear not!" said the chieftain scornfully. "These brethren of Satan fear to leave a circle drawn about them, until it be broken. Why? I know not and care not. It is so, and has always been so. It is part of their accursed faith. Let us bed ourselves under these trees, and sleep."

"He was a harmless old fellow," said Fraser, laughing none the less.

"Harmless?" Tahir Beg snorted in derision. "Had we slept with him, his scorpions might have laid us low ere morning, and then he would have gone his way with all we had, leaving us to recover or die as Allah willed. Harmless! Allah keep us from such harmless ones as he!"

Fraser shrugged and made no further protest, but spread out his blanket beside that of Tahir Beg, and presently was asleep beside the brook.

WHEN FRASER wakened in the morning he left the Kurd to gather figs for breakfast, and took his way toward the house, rather expecting that Ra'sul Majid had taken the brazen peacock and vanished. Entering the doorway, however, he was astonished to find that the old man still sat on his hunkers within the circle, gray head nodding in sleep. The brass bird was untouched.

Ra'sul Majid started, wakened, and seeing Fraser, broke into a whine.

"O blessed Englishman! Release me from this circle, and give me that sacred image—"

Fraser picked up the brazen peacock and pocketed it. The old man cried hastily at him.

"Listen! I will give you riches for it—three fine pearls which I got in Damascus, and which are now sewn into my hat; and twenty goldpieces of Turkish gold! And from Samara, whither I am now bound, I will send you other wealth—"

"I thought you were bound for Persia?" said Fraser—whereat the ancient looked confused and began to stammer. "Peace! I do not want your wealth. As for the circle, let him that drew it there release you from it."

He turned away and departed.

"May Melek Taus curse you, infidel Nazarene!" The anger-quavering voice shrieked after him. "May he follow you with destruction! May your wives dishonor you and—"

The voice died away in a whine of despondency.

When they had finished breakfast, Fraser imparted the old man's offers to Tahir Beg, who listened and nodded complacently.

"I told you the thing had value; so keep it, brother!" he exclaimed. "There is power in it, and it may serve us well. This one-eyed ancient will tell his people that we have it, too, and perchance Al Hudr will try to raid the Hamavand country to get it. Hei! Then we shall have some fun!"

Fraser chuckled. "Little chance of that, I imagine. Go and let the poor devil out of his circle, and let's be on our way. I'll get the horses ready."

Tahir Beg strode off to the house. Before Fraser had half finished saddling up, the chieftain reappeared. Coming to Fraser, he displayed in his hand a cigar-case of tarnished silver, and he held it up with a harsh laugh.

"Now, brother, look you! Judge what our fate would have been had we slept with this *jinni* last night!"

With a quick movement he opened the box and cast it from him. Out of the falling box two large black scorpions fell quivering to the sand. Tahir Beg stamped upon them with his scarlet riding boots, ground them into the dirt; and from the house arose a long wail of curses that shrilled upon the sunrise air.

"Off, and away from the accursed spot!" growled the chieftain.

They cantered forward over the hill trail. Behind them the little valley, with its willows and its house, dropped into the background and was lost; lost, too, was the old rascal Ra'sul Majid—become a vagrant memory, as Bob Fraser carelessly thought.

THEY WERE in the hills, and the high mountains loomed ahead. The road was a steady climb, an unending ascent of small hills only to find larger hills awaiting beyond. The track they followed was a winding and difficult one that threaded the maze of mountains in a most meandering fashion. Tahir Beg, however, seemed to know it by heart.

Bob Fraser was not slow to see that it was this very thing which so marked the tall Kurd apart from others of his race. To most of the mountain men their entire world was bounded by narrow lines; they knew a half-dozen valleys, two or three of the nearer towns, and the few who had been to Mecca were acquainted with the pilgrimage routing. Their cosmos was for the greater part, however, extremely limited, circumscribed by the blinding mountains that shut away the outer world and held them in their forefathers' customs and places.

With Tahir Beg it was different. He was no great traveler; yet he had a cosmopolitan sense of the world; he had ridden much into Persia on lonely forays, had touched with the Russians in the north, had absorbed everywhere. Yet he had not made the pilgrimage.

"Years ago I got me a daughter," he said simply. "Each year I put off the holy duty of going to Mecca, and when the girl was still young, the rest of my family were cut off by a band of Turks. So with the girl I came into the Hamavand country, and stayed, watching her grow and providing for her. If Allah sends me to hell for loving that daughter more than the hot road to Mecca—well and good! But tell me of your father, my brother."

Bob Fraser told quite frankly, extenuating nothing and asking no sympathy. Tahir Beg listened to the recital of Bob's last interview with his father, and broke into roars of laughter; his somewhat Rabelaisan sense of humor saw only the broadest lights, and enjoyed them hugely.

"By the right of Ali!" he swore delightedly, clapping Fraser on the shoulder. "I would like to have seen that old comrade of mine bowled over by his own son! When I see him again, I shall throw that bone in his teeth, eh?"

"You're not likely to see him again," said Fraser dryly. "He's got too much money to look after, these days, to visit this country."

"So? Now listen," returned Tahir Beg, complacently stroking his long yellow mustaches, while his keen eyes kept sharp watch upon the hills: "We rode, your father and I and a dozen horsemen, into Persia. We went to Sulaimanieh, where your father took vengeance on certain enemies and we had hard work to get clear of the town. Then we went on to Sina in Persia, and we had great looting there, and we circled around to Sufiz and stole some girls—"

He checked himself a moment, chuckled, then pursued his subject.

"At Sufiz we met an old woman, from whom Allah had taken away all brain. She was also an infidel, one of those who worship fire; for this reason my men were about slaying her, when your father stopped them. This old woman was given reason for a little space, and told your father that after many years he and I would come together once more and ride as we were then riding. I remember, however, she said that the errand would be a somewhat different one, and that the end of this riding would run bright red with blood of friend and foe. Now, whether that saying applies to you, I cannot say; but I think that the Dispenser will bring your father again to me."

Bob Fraser shrugged his shoulders. "What became of the old woman?" he questioned idly.

"She?" Tahir Beg waved a careless hand. "Oh, my men slew her when your father had turned away, for thereby they obtained grace in the sight of Allah. Now look you to the hill on the right! There are men waiting—they have seen us."

Fraser drove a look at the hill-flank, but could see nothing. A moment later he caught a spat of white smoke among the trees, and a bullet whistled overhead. Tahir Beg laughed, and signaled with his hand.

"Forward and halt not, brother!" he called gayly. "Those are Shuan Kurds, and they are likely to crucify us both if we linger here; so spur hard! Ai, Borak—leap! Over the rocks, Borak!"

His splendid coal-black stallion, Borak or "Lightning" by name, snorted and obeyed. After him spurred Fraser, and the spare horses clattered behind. Another musket banged on the hills, and a slug droned through the air.

"Your welcome to Kurdistan, brother!" shouted Tahir Beg in wild mirth. "Allah be good to us—forward!"

CHAPTER IV

IN THE BEGINNING GOD CREATED THE WHITE PEARL OUT
OF HIS MOST PRECIOUS ESSENCE.—*THE BLACK BOOK.*

A T BAGDAD, which was only two hundred miles
away in a straight line, Bob Fraser had fondly supposed
that all the southern Kurds were alike. So in this, his first riding
with Tahir Beg, he learned that tribe fought against tribe, and
that among the Shuan there was no closed season on Hamavands.

Twice the two men rode hard for life, and once they met on
the road three riders who immediately opened fire with their
homemade Martini-pattern rifles—somewhat to their own
sorrow. Tahir Beg added three good horses to his string that
day, not to mention three rifles and other personal plunder.

None the less, when the two rode quietly into a Shuan village
and demanded hospitality, they were not refused. Accustomed
as he had been to the manners of the Arab folk of the great
Bagdad plain, Fraser was astonished at the simple freedom of
the Kurds—the unveiled and untrammeled women, the primitive simplicity of their home life, and the spotless cleanliness
which seemed to be a passion among them.

Excited by the arrival of the Englishman, for Fraser could
not make these folk comprehend that he was aught else, there
was great telling of tales in the village that night, and feasting
until a late hour. The village mosque was utilized for the occa-

sion, after Fraser had evinced his respect by making the greater ablution and a short prayer; the smoky lights fell upon fierce, childishly curious faces, gayly broidered garments, high conical caps, savage weapons. There were tales of border raids, tales of fantastic adventures in imaginary lands, tales of women and war and magic. One man, a lame brigand who boasted that he had slain thirty Turks and had in his younger days journeyed to Shiraz and Tabriz, gained the floor with a story of an Englishman which he had gleaned in Persian fields.

"He was not a Nazarene, but had been converted to the true faith, and he was a great warrior. With him, they said, rode fifty *jinn,* whom by his talismanic art he had summoned from the depths of the earth, and before them could no warrior stand, and so fleet were their horses that within one parasang they could overtake and slay any who fled from them.

"Now, according to the Imam of Sufiz, who told me the tale, it chanced that a Nazarene *hakim* had opened a hospital at Sufiz and cured many folk. In those days many men preached against the *tib-i-jadid,* the new medicine that was dispensed from bottles and knives; and one day the Nazarene *hakim* and his hospital and his family were mobbed, for that the wife of a Muslim had died under his care.

"Behold now the evident wizardry of Englishmen! The tale is sworn to by the Imam of Sufiz, and sworn by the head of Ali, remember! Even while this mobbing was taking place, the Englishman and his fifty *jinn* fell upon Sufiz, which is a small place, and sacked it utterly. Men were slain and the town was fired, and many girls were carried off; for it is well known that a *jinni* makes practice of carrying off girls and stowing them in underground caverns. And there was great slaughter in Sufiz, during which those who had slain the Nazarene *hakim* were put to the sword by the Englishman without mercy.

"The Imam told me that one of those *jinn,* he who was their master and chief, carried off the daughter of the Nazarene *hakim,* and that the Englishman furthered him in this. When they had finished sacking the town, they rode out and vanished in a great cloud of fire. So if Englishmen have such powers as these, it is not wonderful that they have conquered the Turks, all of whom are dog-brethren!"

THIS TALE met with much applause. Later, however, when Tahir Beg and Fraser were alone in the guest-room that had been assigned them, the chieftain broke out in a long string of fluent curses.

"That lame warrior—you remember his tale, brother?"

"I could not well forget it!" And Fraser chuckled.

"Well, there was some truth in it." Tahir Beg pulled reflectively at his mustache. "Your father was that Englishman, and the *jinn* of whom that fool talked were Gholam Ali Tahir Beg and his fifty men, by Allah!"

"What!" Fraser stared at him. "You mean that?"

"I do, by the beard of Ali! As for that talk about the Nazarene *hakim,* I know nothing of it; but it is true that we sacked that town of Sufiz, your father and I, and the Persians are telling of it to this day! Now to bed, for tomorrow we come into the Hamavand valleys."

So, the tale thus carelessly dismissed, Bob Fraser thought little more of it—except to conclude that Howard Z. Fraser must have made the most of his adventurous opportunities in those early days! However, he was not concerned with the doings of his father, or so he considered.

Upon the following day they wound into the Hamavand country, as Tahir Beg declared it to be. Fraser could see no habitation; but that afternoon they had evidence of it when they encountered two miserable Arab traders. At first four camels only were visible, traveling in pairs; and between each pair two upturned feet. Upon closer approach it became apparent that each Arab was lying full length between his camels, on the joined saddle-bags, for better protection against stray bullets from the hillsides. The traders had incautiously ventured into the Hamavand country, had been stripped of all they had, and had been kicked out with their camels. They went their way, full of whining curses upon all Hamavands, and Tahir Beg chuckled blessings after them.

With the following morning, as they drew down into a long valley, there came a sudden onrush of men from all sides—horsemen who had lain hidden until the last moment, and who now came galloping around them with yells of greeting to Tahir Beg. Fraser was introduced and welcomed.

Hamavands, there, wildest and fiercest of the border folk, delighting in gayly caparisoned horses, in fluttering silks and the peculiar long cloaks of the southern Kurd; their weapons were Turkish rifles, backed by armaments of more savage scimitars and knives, and in their whole bearing a furious ecstasy of life. That the two comrades had ridden alone from Erbil was considered a great feat, and Fraser found himself guested with open hospitality on every hand.

From village to village they went on, and so came at last to the valley where Tahir Beg ruled as chief. Two miles wide and ten in length, abundantly watered, it lay in the heart of the Hamavand country—a valley celebrated in Kurdish song and story as unconquered. At the north was a narrow defile bordered by high spurs of rock, and at the south was a precipitous way, both openings being easily defended by a few men. All the valley was deep with trees and lush grass, where grazed herds of cattle and sheep.

TAHIR BEG'S men came riding to meet their chief—most of them Persian Kurds, like their chief of the Shi'a sect of Islam, and tolerated among the Sunni tribes because of their fighting qualities. They had intermarried, also, and many of them were pure Hamavands; for of late years the religious world of these mountains, like the political world, had been flung into a topsy-turvy confusion.

They were a fine lot of men, hard-riding and hard-fighting mountaineers, and Fraser could well understand the unbounded pride with which Tahir Beg regarded them. They in turn evinced a very real affection and delight in their chief, who typified in his person all the highest attributes of a Kurdish warrior.

There was no permanent village in the valley. Many of the band were scattered through adjoining hills and vales, and the entire valley itself was strewn with low black tents or turf-roofed stone houses that blended inconspicuously into the landscape. One of these latter was the home of Tahir Beg, set so close against a precipitous wall of rock that Fraser would not have guessed their destination had not the White Pearl come forth to welcome them.

Sefid—or "White," as she was commonly termed—was upon Tahir Beg almost before he had dismounted, flinging herself bodily at him in an unashamed burst of affectionate greeting. Fraser was presented, but he could find no words. What little Tahir Beg had said about this daughter of his had not prepared Fraser for the meeting. He had seen many beautiful girls among the Kurds; yet he had seen none so beautiful as this fairy creature!

Dressed in plain white silk, cut in the Arab-fashion of the southern Kurds, Sefid wore none of the elaborate golden ornaments of most hill women. Fraser saw before him a girl unadorned, yet so dazzling in beauty as to leave him dumb and astounded. Her sole jewel was a ring containing a single large pearl—whence, he rightly guessed, her name.

Her bare head was a shimmering golden glory in the sunlight; and under this radiance were delicately chiseled features that reminded Fraser of the almost superhuman fineness of some ancient intaglio. The sun of the hills had not browned her skin, but had lent to it a transparent golden glow of rare health. The startling thing about her, however, was the pair of serious, deeply poised eyes that inspected Fraser with a frank eagerness; they were of a blue so deep as to be black, those eyes, and flecked with gold like the deep goldspecked *lazvard* gem of Khorassan.

"Here is your Englishman!" cried out Tahir Beg, laughing. "And tomorrow we shall see if he can fight with me, eh? Ho, see how the blood comes into her cheeks at that, my brother! She is eager to see Tahir Beg put to earth, eh?"

From the others roundabout, who perfectly understood the allusion, broke a roar of laughter; so that Sefid, confused, turned and ran into the house again to escape from their merriment. One of the nearest warriors clapped Fraser upon the back in good-humored mirth.

"Fight him, Agha Fraser—fight this old wolf and down him! By the lord Ali, we shall be here to cheer you on, those of us who are already married! It is high time this White Pearl of ours were mated, for she is a pearl in name only, and each year her lustre is increased instead of being diminished. Presently there will be bloodshed and wars because of this beauty of hers—and we are minded to let Tahir Beg fight his own wars!"

This gave Fraser some idea of the state of affairs. Seeing that all were watching him, and guessing that his response was being awaited with keen interest, he gazed at Tahir Beg and smiled.

"So that is why you fetched me here—thinking that I would fight you and marry this girl of yours!"

"No, by the right of the lord of the faithful!" swore Tahir Beg. "Yet—"

"Well, I decline!" struck in Fraser quickly. "I can find no lack of men to fight without seeking quarrels among my friends. As for marrying, I intend to choose my own wife. When love comes, I will marry despite father or devil; but until then I am my own master and intend to remain so!"

Fraser could have uttered no words more calculated to delight the independent hillmen, among whom there is little giving in marriage, but much taking.

"Allah upon thee—there spake a man!" shouted the nearest, amid the laughter that greeted Fraser's words. "Hold, Tahir Beg—saw you anything of the Sulaimanieh men in the north? They passed this way a day after your departure."

"I saw them," said Tahir Beg. "And Shaik Nuri has taken unto himself those infidels that worship Shaitan, and has allied himself with them."

These words brought silence, and men gazed one at another with lowered brows.

A M I D   T H E   silence, Tahir Beg brought his guest into the house, where Sefid welcomed them. Now Fraser saw a startling change in her; the simplicity that had marked her attire was gone, and from top to toe she was Persian. She wore upon her radiant hair a skull-cap covered with chains of gold coin and bound with a kerchief of Keshan silk; her garments, from open coat to baggy trousers, were of pale-hued silks; save for crimson slippers, her feet were bare and henna-stained; and about her throat was a necklace of the large golden fishes so fancied by the Kurds of Persia.

"You are welcome here," she said to Fraser, giving him the old-fashioned guesting of the country. "Your service is upon my eyes, and your health, please Allah, is good! You are at home."

Such was the home-coming of Bob Fraser. Nor was it such in empty name only, but in very fact, for from that moment he was as one of the family, and all that Tahir Beg owned was his without the asking.

There followed days of riding and visiting, although to Fraser the happiest times were those spent at home with Tahir Beg and Sefid. The Aorami insisted on taking his guest to meet the other chiefs of the Hamavands, which necessitated covering much ground.

Fraser was not accepted on the strength of his uniform, of his host's vouching, of anything except himself. In this land self-reliance was the all-important thing, and a number of opportunities were made for him to show what he could do in the way of work—even if it were searching for lost cattle on the mountains. Fraser went at it all cheerily.

While they were in the valley of Bazain, visiting with the head chief of the Hamavands, occurred an incident which at the moment Fraser put down to some such testing. From the moment of their arrival in the tent-village, a sulky, ill-conditioned youth by the name of Jafir made himself most objectionable. This attitude came to a head during some religious discussion, when Jafir leaped up and termed Fraser an infidel and worse, following it with a volley of abuse. Fraser calmly picked up a convenient stone and sent it home between the eyes of the youth, who dropped senseless. The hospitable Kurds were scandalized by this affront to a guest, and apologized for it by saying that Jafir was one who had been lately adopted into the tribe; also, it seemed that he had aspired to the hand of Sefid, which somewhat explained his hatred toward the stranger who was a guest in the home of Tahir Beg.

"Let it pass," said Fraser, impassive and undisturbed. "He has suffered more than I."

In the morning it was found that Jafir had disappeared, and with him Fraser's horse. The head chief at once sent out pursuers, but these found no trace of the youth, who had vanished completely.

Fraser thought no more of this incident, and quite forgot the ill-conditioned Jafir in his frank delight in the society of Sefid. Indeed, this girl both puzzled him and aroused in him a great wonder; for one day, as they were talking, she spoke a few words in French.

"Where did you learn those words?" asked the astonished Fraser in French. She stared at him, uncomprehending. When he had repeated the words in Persian, she lifted her brows and laughed.

"Where? I do not know—a thing of childhood, that is all." Yet in her eyes, those strangely deep eyes of lapis lazuli sprinkled with golden flecks, he perceived a troubled look. "Sometimes my tongue slips into it—a few words, or more."

Fraser asked Tahir Beg about this, on the same night. The chieftain listened to him without comment, then made a gesture of careless dismissal.

"Ah! No one hereabouts speaks the tongue of the Franks, brother. I believe it was your father who taught her a few words of it, when he was here in her childhood."

Now, Fraser knew that his father did not understand a word of French, and he realized that Tahir Beg was calmly lying to him. Therefore he held his peace.

Only two men living knew that Sefid was no daughter to Tahir Beg—and Bob Fraser was not one of the two.

CHAPTER V

THREE MEN came riding into the valley from the southland. They bore supposedly genuine letters from chiefs of the Jaf tribes, commending them to the hospitality of the Hamavands; therefore they were well received by Tahir Beg and his folk.

Two were huge black men. They had no tongues, and they were eunuchs, slaves of Uthman Fatteh, who proclaimed himself a Persian merchant. Always they followed him about, standing or squatting impassively behind him, giving him stately salams and obeying his orders with a servile alacrity which made the hillmen stare at them in contempt.

Their presence, with the six spare horses of fine southern breed which they led, made it obvious that the Persian was wealthy and a man of honor. He bore out this conjecture in his appearance—a tall, swarthy, handsome man of forty, dressed magnificently, his sweeping eyes filled with efficiency and a cruel, arrogant energy. An excellent talker, Uthman Fatteh was gladly welcomed as guest by Tahir Beg, whose house was ample. There were tales of Persia and remote hill countries, and often the Persian questioned Fraser about the British, showing no lack of intelligence. Like others, he rejoiced that they ruled Mesopotamia.

"They will have work if they come into Persia," commented the visitor. "Have you heard of that Uthman called Al Hudr, or 'The Green?' They say he has established himself at Penjivan, a great hill place betwixt Sina and Kermanshah."

"I have heard of the place," answered Tahir Beg. He, with Sefid and Fraser, were sitting about the hearth, for the nights were cold. "It is a great mountain of the *jinn* and *div*, and about it live many of those who worship Shaitan. I know the country well, for I was a boy among those mountains; it is not far from Aoraman. And I have heard a little of this Al Hudr, also. Men say that he has collected the devil-worshipers—may their graves be desecrated!—and has wrought them into a strong tribe."

The visitor laughed. He looked at Tahir Beg with shrewd, arrogant eyes, in which seemed to lurk some hidden jest and deep mockery.

"You will hear more of him; men are already talking. It is said that he has sent to Mosul and beyond, bidding all the Yezidis flock to him and join his standard. Also I have heard that he is a great warrior, and they say he has made friendly alliances with many folk not of his accursed faith. There are fools in Islam who would join with him, of course."

"Then, by Allah, there will be riding and slaying in the land!" exclaimed Tahir Beg delightedly. "Although that region is far from here—"

"I believe," put in Fraser quietly, "it is with this man that our friend Shaik Nuri has made alliance. Is not that so, Tahir Beg?"

TAHIR BEG tugged frowningly at his long mustaches, and nodded. The Persian threw Fraser a sleepy look, such a look as one gets from a tawny caged cat, and then gestured in surprise.

"He of the Sulaimanieh Shaiks? Now, that is news! A bad combination for honest men, if true. This Al Hudr, they say, has ridden far—among the Russians in the north, and in Armenia and the Caucasus. He is spoken of as a second Rustam, a hero of heroes—not an ignorant man, but worthy in all ways."

"Perhaps I shall ride to meet him one of these days," Tahir Beg yawned. "If these sayings of yours be true, Persian, he were a right good man to measure swords with."

"Few have measured and lived to tell of it, they say." The eyes of Uthman Fatteh widened for an instant; then the man laughed and rose, bidding them good night.

Fraser sat up late with Tahir Beg, discussing this news. True, the Penjivan district was far in the Persian hills—another little world of its own, girded by mountains and wild tribes; yet if the Sulaimanieh rulers were to join this Al Hudr, here might be the nucleus of a powerful rule.

"By the lord of the faithful!" exclaimed Tahir Beg. "Were it not for the White Pearl, I might ride and join this Al Hudr, for there will be action where he rides! Yet for her sake have I settled down these many years, and until she be married to one of my liking, I shall stay where I am. What think you of my White Pearl, brother?"

"There is only one reply," said Fraser simply. "I have never seen a woman so beautiful—or so worthy of being beautiful. I only hope that she finds—"

The words failed him. The unuttered hope that she might find a husband worthy of her, smote sudden realization into him. To express the hope were a lie, and he knew it. The thought of Sefid married, even to the lordliest Kurd, oppressed him. Yet with what reason? There could be but one answer, and Fraser, suddenly fearful of the truth, shrank from it.

He could hear Sefid, somewhere making *du* for the morrow, singing a Kurdish folksong as she worked. The sound of her voice put fire in his veins; yet, he knew well, he could not for the sake of a woman give his whole life to Kurdistan—not for the sake of the most wondrous woman of earth!

The alternative presented itself coldly. Sefid was of an Aryan stock that had endured through the ages undefiled, purer far than his own; yet she was a Kurdish woman, and back in New York a Kurdish woman would be classed with Armenian or

Turk. How would Sefid take to civilization, she who had naught in her very blood to reconcile her to its ways? Would she not like a mountain eaglet be stifled by its chains? How could he take this woman to a world that might kill her? It was not fair.

TAHIR BEG sat and watched him with thoughtful gaze, and presently broke the silence that had fallen upon them.

"You are thinking, perhaps," he said slowly, "that among the women of America, clad in their strange garments, learning their ways, this White Pearl of mine would stand forth even as a queen among slaves in the marketplace?"

Fraser's lips relaxed in a queer smile. He did not lie to this man.

"No," he answered. "I was thinking, Tahir Beg, that in a strange land and among strange people and customs, the luster of this pearl might be quickly dimmed."

Tahir Beg considered this, and after a moment put out his hand and touched Fraser's knee.

"Listen!" he said gravely. "Among the Turks and Persians the Nazarene women are accursed and shameless creatures in name. Yet they come with their men, these women, and make hospitals and missions; and they are happy in strange lands, among alien peoples, because with them they bring love."

Fraser looked at his host, somewhat astonished by the man's depth, and by the very evident understanding that lay behind the words. But at this moment Sefid appeared, her eyes of gold-speckled lapis looking black in the firelight; she reminded her father that they needed flour, and bade them good night. When she was gone, Tahir Beg sighed.

"Ai, but her beauty smites into a man and looses the sinew of his soul! That flour—I had forgotten it. There is some awaiting me in the camp below the valley—a day's ride there and another day's ride back, and I put off the going because of this Persian guest."

"I'll go after it tomorrow," volunteered Fraser. "I'd be glad of the ride. This Persian is a queer fellow, Tahir Beg, a remarkable man in some ways."

The chieftain grunted. "Aye, and no more merchant than I am, if the truth were known. By the sword of Ali, either that man is a warrior or I am a fool! And his Persian was not smooth; it held an odd accent that was strange to me. Well, Allah made roads for men to use, so why worry? Go after the flour, brother, and take a pack-horse. Or stay! They will load a mule at the camp, so bother not with a led beast."

FRASER DETERMINED to improve on the two-day trip if possible, and with sunrise the following morning he was riding down the long valley. This, at the southern end, debouched into a larger but rather arid valley, little used by the Kurds except for running sheep on the hillsides; and beyond this again was the camp for which Fraser aimed. It was a permanent village of the Hamavands and boasted a small mill run by a mountain stream; upon it many of the nearer camps had come to depend for flour, although the cereal in this form was rather a luxury than otherwise.

He swung briskly along and before noon was past the precipitous way at the valley's south end, and into the farther and more arid valley beyond. Along this he pressed quickly, meeting not a soul yet conscious that from the hills roundabout Hamavand eyes had probably noted his passing.

Already the thought of coming home again was making his pulses leap, the vision of Sefid in the doorway was pulling hard at him; he did not want to be away from her so long. If he traveled all night, he could get home again more quickly—just to be there, just not to be away from there—that was all. She was there, and now he was riding in the wrong direction.

Fraser laughed harshly.

"Perhaps she looks upon me as a barbarian, an outlander; perhaps her heart has been already given to some young Hamavand! And after all, what do I care for the world, for my own people? Dad threw me out, and not without reason; but I've made good over here. I'd like to go back, of course; but how much? Which would weigh the most—going back, or having Sefid for wife? And how badly do I want her? I don't know. Perhaps it's a passing fancy."

He lied to himself there, and deep inside knew the lie.

Shortly before sunset he reached the Hamavand village, where he was known, and a mule was at once prepared for his immediate return. Two Kurds made ready the flour in equal loads, and before he had finished his meal, the mule was waiting.

Long before sunset his homeward road was opening out before him; he had not bothered to obtain a fresh horse, for he was now held down to the speed of the mule. The twilight deepened into evening, and against the blue-black sky glowed and gleamed the sunlit stars; watching them as he rode, Fraser thought anew of Sefid's deeply beautiful eyes like lapis, gold-glinting, as though beneath the blue lay some great fund of radiant fire.

"What is it about her that's taken hold on me?" he wondered, "Not mere sex, surely—not the mere fact that she's a white woman. I've seen plenty others here in the hills. And not her beauty, for I suppose she's actually no more beautiful than others; it's largely in the eye of the beholder, and there's no standard of beauty after all. Gad! I wish Dad were here, so I could tell him I want to marry a Kurdish girl and hear what he'd have to say! I wonder if it's love, the love they tell about in books? Whatever it is, there's a pain at the soul. It's just as Tahir Beg said—"

AT MIDNIGHT Fraser forced himself to pull in his jaded horse and dismount. He did not want to rest; there was a pull at him to go forward, to be back in the stone house, to be near Sefid. Nevertheless he dismounted, let the horse roam and spread out his blanket. The mule he tethered near by among the sparse trees of the arid valley, loaded, since he could not replace the animal's load if he removed it. He meant to rest no more than an hour.

Something went awry in his calculations. He had hoped to be home by sunrise; when he wakened, however, it was in the gray breaking of dawn. Even then he had not wakened of his own will, but had been aroused by a thudding of hooves, a drumbeat of galloping horses; as he sat up, startled, a great rush of shadowy shapes went past him, steadily thundering down the valley.

"Eight or ten of 'em," thought Fraser, rising and staring disgustedly at the eastern sky. "Hm! The false dawn's gone—day's nearly here, and I've been snoring away! Who the devil was galloping so hard?"

He pursued his hobbled horse, found the beast and removed the hobbles. He had just mounted when he paused. From up the valley came a new sound of hooves—a single horse this time, galloping hard as the others had galloped—harder, if anything. Fraser guided his steed into the trail, and glimpsed a vague rider sweeping toward him through the dawning.

Knowing his Kurds and their ways, Fraser shouted his name aloud. To his astonishment the rider did not halt; he merely swerved his horse. Then a rifle spat red, and Fraser caught the whine of a bullet that missed him by inches.

This was a costly error on the part of the other man. Before the rifle-echo had died from the high hillsides, Fraser's automatic gave its curt, ugly bark; and a second time. The American's horse plunged madly to the shots, but as he controlled the animal, Fraser saw the other rider come crashing out of the saddle and drag by one stirrup.

Spurring, he pursued the other beast, caught its bridle, stopped it. Then he leaped to earth and turned over the inert body hanging from the stirrup. He was amazed to find himself staring down at one of Uthman Fatteh's negroid slaves!

What had meant that mad rush of horsemen down the valley at dawn—with this slave pursuing them? Why had the Negro shot at him? Fraser frowned in puzzled wonder. A look at the Negro's horse showed the animal white with lather; evidently the beast had come full gallop for miles. A closer look showed him a hastily mended girth.

"Ah!" The exclamation burst from him. "This fellow was not pursuing them; he was riding with them—his girth broke and he halted to mend it, then was catching up. Why, something must have happened there at home! The Persian and his two men were in flight, headed back south with their spare horses—"

He stooped suddenly. Knotted about the waist of the slave was a bit of cloth, something heavy in it. Fraser ripped it open with his knife, and there before him lay his own brazen peacock, the symbol of Melek Taus!

A vague and startled comprehension spurred at him. He seized the image, thrust it into his pocket, leaped to his own saddle. Disregarding the slave's horse and the mule grazing amid the trees, he drove in his spurs and headed his mount northward at a gallop. Something had happened at home! Had the Persian looted Tahir Beg and fled? Had this brazen peacock been part of the loot? Had aught happened to Sefid?

FRASER SPURRED frantically, confident that he would soon encounter Hamavands in pursuit of the Persian—if indeed it had been the Persian! He met no one, however, until he had come to the precipitous defile that led into the valley of Tahir Beg. As he neared the north end of this, the clear day breaking, he saw men appear in the trail before and behind him, and drew rein at once. Tahir Beg was not here.

"What has happened?" he shouted, seeing the Kurds excited and armed to the teeth.

"We know not!" came the answer. "An hour before day we saw signal fires, and hastened to close the valley, but riders had already gone through."

Amid the rocks above, Fraser saw a Kurd uprise with a wild yell.

"Tahir Beg is at hand! Assembly smokes are rising along the valley. Send for food and the horses, brethren! There will be riding and fighting."

With a ringing of hooves, a medley of yells and shouts and curses, down the narrow path came Tahir Beg and a dozen of his riders. They drew rein at the group around Fraser. The latter saw Tahir Beg as never before—his face livid, a burning madness of fury lighting his gray eyes, words choking in his throat for very rage.

"Water!" croaked the chief, throwing himself from the saddle. "Food—spare horses—every man of you who can ride, come! I have summoned the tribe—they got through, brother?" This to Fraser. "They were not stopped?"

"No." The American displayed the brazen peacock and stuffed it into his saddlebags. "I met one of the Negroes, and took this from him. The others passed me. What has happened, man?"

Tahir Beg jerked forth a great oath and drew a paper from his waistband.

"Read this!" he growled, while the men crowded around. "Read it. By the faith of the prophet, the honor of Ali, the beard of my father, I shall send that son of Shaitan into the bosom of his master!"

Fraser looked at the paper, and found a message written in Persian. The very mockery of that note, to say nothing of its contents, brought a surge of anger into his eyes:

> To Tahir Beg the Aorami, greeting! Thy friend's image of Melek Taus belongs to me, and I have taken it; for this, my thanks to him. Thy daughter is desired by Shaik Nuri, to whom I have taken her. As for thee, come and measure swords when thou wilt, braggart; I have a score to pay thee that has festered these sixteen years! A score against you and Agha Fraser, which I may yet settle against you and Agha Fraser's son. So bring the cub with you.
>
> UTHMAN AL HUDR, Lord of Penjivan.

Fraser glanced up. "Sefid! You do not mean that—"

"The dog-brother carried her away!" cried Tahir Beg hoarse-ly. "In half an hour we shall be after him. Get a fresh horse here, and be ready, for the road is long! Nor will we catch him this side Sulaimanieh."

"Not catch him?" repeated Fraser, aghast. "But then he'll be in safety, and Sefid—"

"Not in the seventh pit of hell will he reach safety from me!" roared Tahir Beg. And somehow the words seemed no boast— simply the literal truth.

CHAPTER VI

"OF PARADISE I CANNOT SPEAK PROPERLY, FOR
I WAS NOT THERE."—SIR J. MANDEVILLE.

HOWARD Z. FRASER came to Samara in record-breaking time and arrived without any fuss and feathers. He was escorted directly to the house occupied by the general in command of the district, and sent in his card. Winkler, who had arrived with him, was left in the anteroom when Fraser was ushered into the presence of the general. It was characteristic that he shook hands calmly, waved aside all proffered hospitality and came straight to the point.

"They told me at Bagdad that you'd have news of that boy of mine. Have you any?"

The General nodded. "As soon as I was apprised of your coming, Mr. Fraser, I sent to Mosul with orders to find Lieutenant Fraser. He was last heard of at Erbil, where he had gone with Captain Harrowgate to explore—"

"I know all that," broke in Fraser crisply. "What's the latest?"

The General frowned.

"I regret to say, sir, that Mr. Harrowgate died there of fever. Your son has disappeared. We have now occupied Erbil, but the officer in command there reports that your son left the place some weeks ago, and nothing is known of his destination except that he rode to the south. He is not at any intervening town.

It appears obvious that he was either waylaid by brigands or fell into the hands of roving Kurds—"

"You've not pacified the Kurds, then?" demanded Fraser shrewdly.

The General hesitated. "There seems to be a good deal of unrest and trouble among the hills, Mr. Fraser. We are heavily occupied in taking over the administration—"

"I see," said Fraser, rising. "Well, I'll not detain you. I appreciate very much what you've done, and I think I'll look around for myself. No objection, I suppose, to my having a look for the boy?"

"Er—you don't mean up-country, I trust?"

"Naturally, I do," said Fraser dryly. "I don't imagine Bob is here in town."

"But my dear sir! It's quite unheard of, really; to guarantee your safety would require a larger force than I am able to spare at the present moment—"

"See here, General," said Fraser confidently, "you're on the wrong tack! I don't want to parade through Kurdistan with a bunch of Sikh soldiers at my tail, singing out to all the folks to get out of the way of Howard Z. Fraser! I was here years ago, and I've got some mighty good friends up in the hills—or hope I have. I've been picking up the language once more, and can handle it pretty decently—Persian too.

"Winkler, my man, is a good scout, and I can depend on him. We'll appreciate your help in getting hold of some horses— that's all. I'll hire a few men and slide along into the hills like any other traveler. I don't look for a bit of trouble; all I'm worried about is that boy of mine, and I expect he's up in the hills somewhere chinning with the Kurds."

"Let me at least furnish you with the men."

Fraser objected, politely but firmly.

"Thanks, General; but I'll be frank enough to say that I'd rather hire a few hillmen myself and depend solely upon my own judgment. I'll go straight to Sulaimanieh and Halabja, then work north if I discover nothing. Have you occupied those places yet?"

"No," said the General. "One or two of the *shaiks* are here, conducting negotiations, but I'm waiting to look over the scene in person; there are so many conflicting stories that it is impossible to issue judgment from a distance. And we must be just, you know."

"That's a British fallacy," said Fraser, grinning. "Then you've no objection to my going ahead?"

"I suppose not, although I hardly approve it, sir. I suppose you've made no arrangements about stopping here, so I'll be very glad to place a house at your disposal. If you find yourself in lack of anything, I hope you'll call on me; you had best mess with us here, too, for you'll find little decent food in the town."

FEELING AS though he had come a good many thousand miles for nothing, Fraser allowed himself to be escorted to a small, clean house where he and Winkler were presently domiciled. Winkler heard the report of the General in his usual silence and had no comment to offer. The great dusty plain frightened Winkler, and so did the people; but he remained quite unruffled outwardly, tried hard to learn a little Kurdish, and maintained a serene faith in the abilities of his very confident master.

Fraser was confident enough, beyond doubt. Yet he found that the years had dimmed his perceptions; he was unable to tell at a glance whether a man was an Arab or a southern Kurd, whether a passing tribesman was of the Jaf or Bajlan; more important, he found it hard to tell from bazaar talk whether the speakers were of the Sunni or Shi'a sect. Trying to convince himself that this mattered little, Fraser became more self-assured than ever. He searched out all who came from the hills, and talked with them, but none had news of his son. However, word went abroad of him of his errand, so that he felt sure that

before long some one who had heard of Bob would also hear of him, and would come to him. Meantime he began to select a half-dozen men to accompany him into the hills.

When the messenger of Kadir came to him, Fraser had picked and engaged two men; this, as it turned out, was important. The two were brethren of some obscure tribe of Kurds in Persia. They had been fighting and adventuring to Mecca and home again, enlisting with the British forces en route, and were now free to accompany him. Their names, taken ironically from some effect of the evil eye upon the Arabs, whom they despised, were A'in and Ma'un. They were always in company, these two men; and unlike most Oriental brethren, they held a strong affection for each other.

Having hired them, Fraser, five days after his arrival, was strolling past the great golden-domed mosque that marks Samara from afar,—the holy mosque that is the outstanding building of this dust-hued city on the high cliff above the Tigris,—when the one-eyed messenger touched his arm.

Fraser was marveling at the crowds of holy *Sayyids* and groaning beggars which filled the place; indeed the beggars of Samara are a byword throughout Islam. The city is one of the historic and holy places of the Moslem faith, for in one of its cellars vanished from sight the twelfth Imam, hailed by the Shi'a sect as the head of Islam, and who shall come again to earth as the expected Mahdi. The fact that he has come several times does not affect the sacredness of the prophecy. During the past thousand years Samara has not only been holy; it has enjoyed an unequaled reputation for wickedness, depravity and all evil.

WHEN A man touched Fraser's arm, therefore, he turned impatiently to rid himself of some beggar. Then he halted. The man at his side was old, much scarred, and one eye was gone in a hideous red weal. The other eye glowed like a living topaz, yellow and lurid.

"You are Agha Fraser?" said this old man in Kurdish.

"So I am called," admitted Fraser with a gleam of hope. "You seek me?"

"He whom I serve sent me to find you. He has word of one who is lost."

"Ah!" exclaimed Fraser quickly. "Whom do you serve, old man?"

"I am Ra'sul Majid, and I serve one named Shaik Kadir, who is of the holy family of Sulaimanieh. If it be your will, *agha*, I can lead you to him now."

"Lead on, in the name of Allah!"

As he spoke, Fraser felt thankful that Winkler had remained at home, for Winkler was anything but happy among the natives, and was ever advising caution.

The one-eyed ancient led him through the maze of shops behind the mosque and into a small room where sat a gray-bearded old man whose face was the epitome of cunning, cruelty and all uncharitableness. His immense headgear, wound about with green kerchiefs, denoted his tribe and sanctity; the long and voluminous robes that cloaked him told plainly of his Sulaimanian origin.

At sight of Fraser a cruel gleam shot athwart the countenance of Shaik Kadir—a gleam that spelled a most unholy recognition. It was gone at once, however, and he greeted his guest with a respectful *marhaba* and effusive compliments. Fraser glanced at him sharply, and felt a very dim stirring of memory, but failing to recall that evil face, gave all his attention to the news of Bob.

WHEN HOST and guest were seated, the one-eyed brought a tray of cigarettes and sherbets, and Shaik Kadir began to say what was in his mind.

"I heard of your affliction, Agha Fraser, and my heart was sad for the grief of a father. It chanced that only yesterday, this man, Ra'sul Majid, arrived here from the north with many curious tales to relate. When he had told his tales, I knew that he must have met your son. Therefore I sent him for you, that you might understand his tale to be no lying story told for reward, but entire truth.

"Allah upon thee, Ra'sul Majid! Tell the truth alone, in the name of the Compassionate!"

The topaz eye of the scarred ancient blazed with deeper hues. It fastened upon Fraser in a glittering gaze that did not quail before the keen scrutiny of the American.

"Agha, I speak that which I saw, in the name of Allah!" As he spoke, he produced a metal case and began to toy with it. "I cure the hurt of scorpions, and men know of me from Saloniki to Samarcand, for through all countries have I traveled; sixteen times have I performed the greater pilgrimage, and eight times the lesser. Upon a certain day I was passing through a village beyond Kirkuk, to the north, when folk called to me and in the name of God implored me to visit an Englishman who there lay dying."

"Dying!" repeated Fraser, and his iron features changed slightly.

"So they said, *agha*. Out of my compassion I went in to the Englishman, and found him tossing with the fever of scorpion-stings. I took the oil of black scorpions and looked to his hurts, *agha;* and two days I remained there watching over him. In the end I knew that Allah had restored him to life and enjoyment."

As he spoke, Ra'sul Majid opened his case, and two black scorpions leaped out upon his arm, writhing and striking furiously. If Fraser had been expected to show fear, there was disappointment for the others; he had seen these tricks many a time, and guessed that the stings of the insects had been nipped away. Presently Ra'sul Majid gathered his two pets into the box again.

"That deed shall be well rewarded," said Fraser quietly. "What learned you of my son?"

"Little, *agha*. He traveled alone, and seemed a proud man, quite without fear. While I sat by him, he told me that he was going to Sulaimanieh, but of his business there he would say nothing. So I gave him letters to certain holy men of the place, that he might not arrive there without friends."

"That was well done," said Fraser, dry humor in his voice. "Sulaimanieh was ever a town of ill repute, and strangers who come unrecommended gain little welcome there."

"If it be your will to go thither," said Shaik Kadir, "I will give you letters under my own seal, and send with you certain of my own men under the command of Ra'sul Majid. My brother's son, Shaik Nuri, is ruler of the district, and you shall be to him as a brother."

Fraser did not pause to consider. It was nearly a score of years since he had been in Sulaimanieh, and in those days he had not been there as a welcomed guest. It was quite plain that Kadir had not recognized him, however, and he had no fears for his own safety; since these men were doing everything possible to retain their rule under the British administration, they would certainly see that he was fully protected. So he reasoned swiftly.

"Allah will requite you for this kindness," he said. "Will your men be ready tomorrow?"

"After the early prayer they shall be at your abode," promised Kadir.

"Then I must see about horses and supplies." Fraser rose, and turned to Ra'sul Majid. "I shall not attempt to requite your charity toward my son, for charity is its own reward. Out of respect to your good will, however, I shall have a gift for you tomorrow. May Allah be gracious to you all! *Wa'l salám!*"

He departed, chuckling to himself; evidently sixteen years had wiped away all memory of him among the Sulaimanians!

"Wa'l Salám!" repeated Shaik Kadir ironically when Fraser had gone. "And here ends the matter—eh? Dog of a Nazarene! Now you have come into the net, and it is twined around you, and the matter shall end otherwise than as you look for! Draw near, Ra'sul Majid, and listen to me."

THE ONE-EYED plucked at his dirty beard, lighted a cigarette, and listened to the master of evil who sat and mouthed furious curses, the while he related a passion-trembling tale.

"When I was a younger man, this same infidel dog was in Sulaimanieh—aye, the same man, although he deemed that I did not know him again after all the years! There were Turks in the city in those days, and the *wali* plundered this man somewhat, and when he complained, gave him fifty blows of the bastinado."

"Wah!" ejaculated Ra'sul Majid. "He is not the man to be bastinadoed lightly!"

Kadir cursed again. "He went away, but one day he came back, disguised and unnoted, and with him some filthy Persian Kurds. At night they came to the palace of the *shaik,* my brother, and slew all the guards without a sound, so that before any man awakened they had come into the harem and had taken all of us prisoners, together with the women. There they held us while this infidel dog defiled the women by unveiling their faces, taunting us the while; and he took all the jewels, saying that so he would repay himself for the plundering."

"Wah!" said Ra'sul Majid again.

"And then," pursued Kadir, mounting to a venomous height in his interspersed curses, "he took his pipe-stem and struck all of us in the face with it, thus to repay the bastinado![1] Then he and his got away out of the city and were no more heard of."

"Now I understand," said Ra'sul Majid thoughtfully, "why you sent me for him. Hey! What shall I do to him on the way north?"

"Get the black tin box that is beside my bed."

The one-eyed rose and departed. Presently he returned, bearing the tin box in question. Kadir opened it with a key and took out certain objects.

"Take him safely to the city, and on the first night he sleeps in the palace of Shaik Nuri, bestow this in his room where he will see it." He handed the one-eyed a stained kerchief of silk, broidered with Persian words. "It was one he wore that night, and dropped in his flight. He will remember it again. Then take this letter to Shaik Nuri, who will obey it."

"You do not wish me to kill him?" Ra'sul Majid looked grieved.

"Not until the time appointed—for I desire to be there to see," said Kadir grimly. At this the one-eyed looked more content. He knew with what manner of master he dealt.

---

1   A blow with such an object is the deepest insult in the East.

CHAPTER VII

"IF A MAN STEAL THE WIFE OF HIS NEIGHBOR... SHE
IS THE BOOTY OF HIS HAND."—*THE BLACK BOOK.*

WHEN HOWARD Z. FRASER left the desolate sandy plain behind him and found the mountains rising on every hand, and the great snow-peaks towering into the eastern horizon, he was one of the happiest men in Mesopotamia.

That Bob was somewhere in the hills, he felt convinced; therefore his worry had been greatly lessened. Once more he had a horse between his legs; the sonorous Kurdish was at his tongue's end; he was leading his own men into the venturesome hills; overnight, as it were, much of his youth had returned to him. Sixteen years had slipped from his shoulders.

It was nearly a score of years since Fraser had ridden over this land, a young man. In those days the country had been different—bloodily ruled by the Turk, with an Osmanli fair game for every hillside rifle. Then Fraser had come into the country much as a gunman might have come into the mining camps of Nevada in early days; a man might be his own law; he might do absolutely what he wished, so long as he had the force of character to back his own play to the utmost. He must back it absolutely, fearlessly.

Fraser had done all this. Then he had gone home to civilization. The clouding years had come creeping about him and had passed. Now he was back again on Kurdish soil; and in the queer fashion that is part of life's irony, the memory of his earlier days here had become dimmed until only the high lights were left. He had absolutely forgotten many details, many things that a lesser man would have remembered; the intervening years had been busy, crowded with great deeds and events, and had wiped from his mind a great deal that would have given him no pride in the recollection.

Now as he rode into the hills, something of the old head-strong, freebooting spirit stirred again in his blood. He began to think less of his son and more of himself; there was an organization to be upbuilt; there was plunder of oil and minerals to be grabbed—mighty things, yet unguessed of by most men, lay potential in this country. With each day the predatory lines in Fraser's face grew deeper. Big things lay all around him for the doing. So it was, too, that he forgot much of the past. Often a man can be most successful when forgetting his misdeeds and even his crimes—until they arise to smite him into a shocked remembrance.

FRASER MADE Ra'sul Majid his constant companion, taking keen delight in the shameless rascality, lust and utter deviltry of the man—-who, as he discovered, was by no means so old as he appeared. Fraser rather left poor Winkler to his own devices these days; and Winkler, seeing the change that was upon his master, grew more silent and impassive each hour. To Winkler it seemed that they were rushing upon a certain disaster of some sort.

The men furnished by Ra'sul Majid were bold ruffians, lazy rufflers who dealt in high words and great curses. They did not mix well with the two proud hillmen first engaged, A'in and Ma'un. These brethren kept aloof, and were always together. Winkler rode much with them; they helped him to struggle with the language, and he found them dependable.

Matters stood thus when one afternoon Ra'sul Majid pushed on ahead with five of his men; suddenly and without explanation they rode out of sight, spurring hard. Two remained, besides A'in and Ma'un, and these two could give no reason for their leader's hurried departure.

"If I might suggest, sir," said Winkler, riding beside Fraser, "it might not be well to trust that one-eyed fellow—"

"Nonsense, Winkler! You don't understand these people." And Fraser laughed.

"Quite true, sir. But A'in was telling me that the other night he heard Ra'sul Majid talking and laughing with one of those ruffians, and it was about you. Ra'sul Majid showed the other man something that he kept wrapped up in his waistcloth, sir, and they both laughed very heartily. A'in said that there was something crooked—"

"Winkler, for the love of heaven, stop croaking! The old man is a scorpion-charmer; he has a pair of tame black scorpions, and that was what A'in saw. Tell those two fool Persians to mind their own business."

Winkler told them nothing of the sort, however. For the first time in many years he began to fully realize that his master was a harsh man, self-centered and unbothered by ethical principles, whose belief in the right of the strongest was untempered by any mercy or regard for the rights of others.

Camp was made, and darkness had fallen when Ra'sul Majid and his party showed up. Winkler sat a little apart beside the two brethren; Fraser greeted the one-eyed with a laughing shout, and when the riders came into the firelight, it was seen that with them was an extra horse, and a vague shape was tied in the saddle.

Between the two brethren passed a low, growling word that Winkler could not understand; but he understood the half-breathed oaths, the hands clutching knife-hilts, the sudden storm of passion in their faces, and he sought the cause. It lay in the tied figure, he perceived.

Ra'sul Majid and one of his men went to the figure, pulled it from the saddle and dragged it to the fire. There was a loosening of ropes and swathing-cloths. A woman was revealed, a young Kurdish woman who stared about her wide-eyed in affright. Her wrists were still bound at her back.

"Hello!" exclaimed Fraser. "What does all this mean, Ra'sul?"

His topaz eye glittering brightly; the other rubbed his hands and chuckled.

"A new wife, *agha*—I have got me a new wife. Is it not written in the holy book that if a man steal the wife of his neighbor, she is the booty of his hand? I have had this one marked down for some months now."

Winkler sat motionless, frozen with horror. Across him leaned A'in, speaking to his brother in a low, astonished voice which vibrated hatred and passion.

"By Ali! He is of the Yezidis, this old one—so are they all, the accursed!"

"Be silent," answered Ma'un, "and see what Agha Fraser will do."

THE WOMAN had seen Fraser, had seen him gazing down at her. A twist of incredulous anguish contorted her whole body as she flung herself at him in the dust.

"Lord!" she wailed brokenly. "Save me from this evil *jinni*—he slew my man."

Her voice fell into great heaving sobs that wrenched her body convulsively. Fraser frowned and turned away.

"Customs of the country," he observed. "Ra'sul, you damned scoundrel, I've a notion to make you take that woman back!"

The one-eyed laughed softly. Winkler listened in growing amazement.

"You would not interfere with the law of our prophet, *agha*. No Englishman would do that! It is my business, not yours."

"Right enough, I suppose," answered Fraser. "You'll take her with us?"

"Certainly, *agha*."

One of the Persian brethren spat in the dust. But Winkler came to his feet and stumbled forward to the side of Fraser.

"You—you can't mean that, sir?" he cried in English.

"Hello!" Fraser turned and looked at him curiously. "Worked up, are you? Forget it, Winkler; you'll have to close your eyes to a lot of things in this country."

Winkler trembled violently. The woman, crawling in the dust, had touched his foot with her head, sensing him, perhaps, as a protector. The touch sent a quivering shudder through him, broke down his self-control.

"You mustn't say that, sir!" His voice was fluid, his words running queerly.

"Don't be a fool, Winkler," cut in the cold, incisive tones of Fraser.

"Fool?" repeated Winkler, drawing a deep breath. "Fool?"

He stopped and began to fumble with blind fingers at the cords binding the woman. A snarl broke from Ra'sul Majid; and his men closed in about the two, sensing the meaning of Winkler's actions if not his words.

Then suddenly each figure stiffened and turned, motionless. The two Persian brethren had vanished, but out of the darkness came the drawling voice of A'in.

"Quiet, ye followers of Shaitan! Touch not the Nazarene or the woman, lest ye want a bullet swiftly! Agha Fraser, these men be no honest Kurds, but Yezidis and worshipers of the devil. Leave them and come with us."

"Allah upon you!" cried Fraser furiously. "Winkler, leave that woman alone."

"You go to hell," snapped Winkler, loosing the cords at last. He pulled the woman to her feet, and as he stood irresolute, the voice of Ma'un came from the darkness.

"Send her here, Nazarene. Join us quickly."

A HOWL broke from Ra'sul Majid, a howl of imprecation and fury. Fraser made a step forward, and one of the men was thus emboldened to snatch out his knife; but the blast of a shot split the darkness, and the man fell forward dead.

"Careful!" cried A'in. "He who moves dies—move not, Agha Fraser!"

Under the unseen menace even Fraser stood silent, his face working with anger. Then he lifted his voice at Winkler.

"You fool, this is suicide! Come back here before it's too late."

Winkler, at the edge of the firelight, turned for a moment.

"I hadn't thought it of you, sir," he said, a pathetic dignity in his voice. "I'm sorry to leave you this way, sir; but I can't stop now—we'll have to take this woman home. You've a heart of stone, sir—a heart of stone! Your razors are in the brown bag."

He vanished into the darkness. Presently there sounded a trampling of hooves that lessened on the night. The riders were gone. Ra'sul Majid flung himself to the ground and heaped dust upon his hair amid a wailing drone of curses.

Fraser stood staring into the night, a sudden chill upon him. He could not realize what had so moved Winkler; he could not visualize himself as he was in that hour. In fact, he believed what Ra'sul Majid cunningly inferred—that the two Persians had stolen the woman for themselves. Fraser was forced to laugh at the thought that these men of Sulaimanieh could be idolaters, worshipers of Melek Taus—had not the Sulaimanians always been famed for their fanaticism and bigotry? In Fraser's mind the whole affair was a confused jumble. Winkler was gone, and he felt sorry for Winkler, a child among these barren hills.

"Damned fool!" thought Fraser roughly, trying to curb his own anxiety. "He's smashed up everything; let him take the consequences!"

So he turned to Ra'sul Majid and tried to make the best of things. He felt, suddenly, sick at soul and empty of heart. It was impossible that he should realize the truth of his position— betrayed, with enemies around him, walking blindfolded into the trap of an ancient hatred; and yet some far inward misgiving must have seized upon him. The cold chill of the night entered into him. He had the unwonted sensation of having committed some hideous and awful mistake, done beyond recall; yet he could not put his finger on just the error. To him it seemed that Winkler was the fool.

"Might have taken the woman's part with him," he reflected, "but the whole bunch would have turned on us and murdered the woman to boot! Finding Bob is more important to me than protecting Kurdish women—but it's dreadful that Winkler's gone. Those damned Persians may do anything to him."

THE DEAD man was buried ere dawn, and Fraser went his way beside the sullen Ra'sul Majid. He had previously questioned the one-eyed regarding a certain Tahir Beg, but Ra'sul said that he had not heard the name in years, and thought the Kurd chieftain had died in some raid. Seeing no guile in this, Fraser accounted his old comrade dead, and asked no further.

They were entering the Jaf country now, and reaching for Sulaimanieh. Toward the middle of the afternoon following Winkler's defection, they sighted a horseman who was riding hard toward the south. He hailed them with a shout of recognition and drew rein, glancing curiously at Fraser. Ra'sul Majid hastened forth to meet him, with some hasty speech. From the horseman broke ejaculations of astonishment; then the two came slowly in toward the other riders.

"Who is this man?" demanded Fraser.

"A courier from Shaik Nuri," answered the horseman himself. "The land is red, lord! The accursed Hamavands have risen against Sulaimanieh, and all roads are closed; three of us left the city to ride with word to Shaik Kadir at Samara, and I alone got through."

"The Hamavands!" The word conjured up before Fraser old memories, memories of Tahir Beg and the wild riding of former days. Then he sighed. "Well, they have sacked the city before and may do it again. Shall we turn to Halabja?"

The courier shrugged. "All the hills are in tumult, *agha.* Uthman al-Hudr has fallen upon Halabja and the Jaf tribes like a whirlwind."

"Who is this Al Hudr?" questioned Fraser, frowning.

They told him of the chieftain, a man who had banded to-gether the devil-worshipers of Persia, who was setting up a new rule for himself—a man already famed as a warrior and daring leader of men. In glowing colors they painted him, a lord of chivalry and romance.

Shaik Nuri, it appeared, was holding Sulaimanieh against the Hamavands, while Uthman was coming to aid him. Fraser listened awhile, then made his decision.

"This Al Hudr seems to be such a man as I would meet. Let us ride to Halabja and meet him, then turn with his force and sweep Sulaimanieh clean of the Hamavands. Eh, Ra'sul?"

The topaz eye of the old man gleamed balefully.

"Good, Agha Fraser," he assented quickly. He was quick of wit, this one-eyed, and saw at once what was to be done. "To Halabja, brethren! And you who ride to Samara, spare not your horse, for Shaik Kadir must know these things and gain the ear of the British swiftly."

The courier waved his hand and rode southward.

Now Ra'sul Majid conferred with his brethren, then took up the trail again; and before sunset they struck, off the road by a winding hill track that smote straight at the heart of the looming Karadagh precipices. The party camped that night fireless, under a bitter wind that drove chill out of the mountain clefts; and Fraser wondered whether Winkler lived or died, but had no answer.

Through the mountains they went, avoiding any sign of habitation, slinking like thieves by hill and dale, with one man riding far ahead and another to the rear, lest the Jaf riders swoop upon them. They saw no danger, however, and so came at last to their goal, winding down upon the fertile plain of Shari-zur—once despoiled and desolated by the Turk, the wondrous "Amber Flower," richest beauty of the Persian realm.

Beyond lay the great wall towering into the sky, the wall that was the Aoraman Mountain, and twenty miles away across the plain lay Halabja on its rising slope—Halabja, where the powerful Jaf chieftains ruled by the strong hand. Gone were the black tents and herds, only clouds of dust told Fraser that men rode about the valley. One of these dust-clouds approached and gave birth to a dozen wild horsemen who discharged rifles into the air with loud shouts as they charged down upon the travelers.

Yells of recognition greeted Ra'sul Majid and his companions, however; and this swift recognition gave Fraser the first hint of something amiss. Closing about the newcomers, exchanging shouts in a tongue strange to Fraser, the whole band urged forward; their aim was a reach of willows beside a brook, and here appeared to be a camp in a deserted Jaf village.

All about lay plunder and panoply of war—a vast melange of gloriously woven carpets, of horses, leather trunks, a few morose prisoners, dashing hillmen, women slaves. As Fraser reined in his horse and dismounted with the others before one of the houses, realizing that they must have come to the camp of the famed Al Hudr, he suddenly observed an object tied to the tail of his horse. It was a silken kerchief—a soiled, stained kerchief of bright silks, dark with old blood.

FROM FRASER'S lips burst a choked exclamation. He seized the fluttering thing, staring at it dumbfounded. It brought back to him ancient days long forgotten—wild deeds, lusty ways of youth; for it had been a gift from the hand of Tahir Beg, woven to order, and there was none other like it in all the land.

He looked about for Ra'sul Majid, but the one-eyed had disappeared. About him had closed the wild riders, regarding him from fierce eyes, unfriendly faces. He clapped a hand to his automatic—and found that it had vanished. The leather holster had been cut clear away.

"Well!" chuckled a voice in Persian. "Dost remember me, Agha Fraser?"

Fraser whirled to meet the keen gaze of Al Hudr; and at sight of the chieftain a startled word broke from him. Remember—did he remember! And now, among the ring of fierce faces, he glimpsed the scarred and evil grin of Ra'sul Majid leering at him. Trapped! The thought vibrated within him dreadfully.

"Welcome, Agha Fraser," went on Uthman, the Green One, a tigerish smile playing about his stern features. "It seems that fate has brought you here; you were being taken to Sulaimanieh to serve the vengeance of another, but you have come into my hand instead. Praise be to Melek Taus! I see that you remember me, after these sixteen years!"

Fraser collected himself with an effort.

"I remember you," he said. "You have changed your name, but I remember you."

Then fell silence, while the two men gazed each at the other in a steady eye-grip. At length Al Hudr laughed grimly.

"Well, it is I who am dealing forth punishments this time!" he said, and gestured to his men. "Bind this Nazarene and throw him into the stable yonder, until I am ready to deal with him."

CHAPTER VIII

"YE KNOW NOT WHETHER YOUR PARENTS OR YOUR
CHILDREN BE OF GREATER USE TO YOU. THIS IS
AN ORDINANCE FROM GOD."—*THE KORAN.*

A SLAVE-GIRL CAME to Sefid and squatted down to gossip over a cigarette. She was a pert little slave, this, captured by the Jaf in some raid and taken with the rest of the booty by Al Hudr when he gleaned the valley of Sharizur. The apartments allotted to Sefid were on the upper floor of Al Hudr's house in the deserted Jaf village, now deserted no longer!

"Our lord has taken a new captive, an Englishman, they say. Have you seen him?"

Sefid shook her head and nibbled at the sherbet before her. A hanging lamp of brass lighted the apartment; about her was every luxury which could be provided by a warrior chief. But the doors were bolted, and were guarded by black slaves, dumb men, eunuchs.

"A young man?" she queried, hanging on the answer.

"Nay, a man of fifty. There is a curious tale to it. Shall I tell you the tale?"

Sefid nodded, and relaxed carelessly; her interest in the Englishman was gone, now that she knew it was not *her* Englishman. However, she knew also that this pretty slave was scarce-

ly to be trusted—a snaky little thing; and she kept herself well
in hand, feigning a languorous ease.

Sefid was already thinking of escape.

Almost from the first she had realized that the danger which
threatened her was not immediate. Seized from her bed, trussed
and bound to a horse, captived and helpless, she had heard Al
Hudr's statement that he was taking her to be the bride of Shaik
Nuri, and that he was taking the brazen peacock for himself.
Indeed, it was to execute this double theft that he had come
into the Hamavand country. Sefid could not but admire the
man's cool audacity and bravery. There was a touch of knight-
hood and chivalry about him.

And to this extent only. Sefid laughed now to think of how
Al Hudr had fooled Shaik Nuri, for the redoubtable Persian
had changed his mind with daylight. One of his slaves was
gone, and with him the brazen peacock; therefore, not to return
empty-handed, he decided to keep Sefid for himself.

Already his full force was sweeping fire and sword through
Sharizur toward Halabja, and he could not well send her to his
mountain fastness. So, meeting certain of his men outside Sulaimanieh, he consigned Sefid to their care and then entered
the city. He boldly told Shaik Nuri that he had failed, that Tahir
Beg was on his heels—which was true—and that Nuri would
have to withstand the Hamavands until he had taken Halabja
and could return to his aid. He had then ridden off to join his
rabble of an army, and was given no time to molest Sefid.
Indeed, she gathered that for the present some religious difficulty stood as a safeguard betwixt her and the chieftain.

Shaik Nuri, left to bear the brunt of the storm, promptly sent
off some of his treasures and women to the Penjivan hills, gathered what men he could, and tried to escape on the heels of Al
Hudr. In this he was too late. Tahir Beg struck like a thunder-
bolt; Shaik Nuri turned to bay like a trapped wolf; and the
Hamavands were checked.

Al Hudr, meantime, led his force through the vale of Sharizur, smote the Jaf villages hip and thigh and besieged their

chiefs in Halabja. About taking that petty town Al Hudr cared nothing. He had amassed quantities of loot and slaves through the valley, and if he lingered here, the whole gathered Jaf tribesmen would be on him. So he kept Halabja in a state of siege while he dispatched his loot to safety. And on this evening Sefid had been told that with dawn she would be sent off with a caravan bound for Penjivan.

SEFID, WHO seemingly had accepted the situation with remarkable coolness, had schemed to shoot Al Hudr and try to get away should he come to extremes with her. Otherwise she felt confident that Tahir Beg would rescue her. Perhaps Bob Fraser figured somewhat in her confidence also.

"Sixteen years ago, they say, this Englishman was here," the slave girl was saying over her languid cigarette. "His name is Agha Farizur."

"Fraser!" exclaimed Sefid, then relaxed again, giving no sign of the thrilling wonder that had vibrated through her brain. "Sixteen years ago?"

"Yes; he has come now to seek a son who is lost. By Allah, these infidels are queer! Why should a man seek a son who can take care of himself? Well, sixteen years ago our lord Al Hudr was but a young man, beardless, a very gazelle in beauty, and he was a member of a band of raiders captained by this Agha Farizur. The infidel overbore him in some dispute, and there was a fight in which our lord was beaten, and fled."

The slave paused to suck at her cigarette—a dramatic pause, for the tale was not done. Sefid was listening with a bored air which concealed a keen interest.

"Is not thy chattering ended yet, magpie?" she inquired listlessly.

"Not yet, lady; listen, now! Our lord sought the life of Agha Farizur, who captured him and then ordered him to be basti nadoed until he was close to death; after this he allowed our lord to go free in contempt. That was all. But behold, how Allah dispenseth justice and ruleth the ways of destiny! Sixteen years after, our lord is very powerful, and this infidel dog comes wandering into his hand like a bird into the net of the fowler! True, they say that our lord is an infidel likewise and worships Shaitan, but what of that?" The girl shrugged lightly and laughed. "Allah alone knoweth all things! Perchance Allah sent that evil one-eyed dog Ra'sul Majid to lead the infidel hither by guiles. I think Shaik Nuri, or his family, had somewhat to do with it, but that is all I know."

Now, Sefid lay back among her cushions and closed those deep-blue eyes of hers, but in thought, not in languid idleness.

Tahir Beg and Fraser had spoken of meeting the one-eyed Ra'sul Majid, and she did not miss this clue. Also she knew very well that Bob Fraser's father had been the old companion-in-arms of Tahir Beg. Therefore it was certain that Tahir Beg had been concerned in the bastinado which had been given Uthman al Hudr sixteen years ago—a thing the Persian had not forgotten. The conclusion that Uthman's vengeance was now destined to strike Tahir Beg as well as Fraser, was obvious.

Sefid thought over these matters, then sat up. She idly twisted a ring upon her finger—a great blazing sapphire of Khorassan, sent her that very day by Al Hudr as a gift. Her gold-shot eyes fastened speculatively upon the slave-girl.

"I would like to see this Englishman," she said carelessly, "for I have never seen one, and this tale interests me. Bring him to me and let me speak with him."

"Allah!" ejaculated the slave hastily. "He is kept in the stable, bound and guarded."

"What is that to me?" said Sefid languidly. She drew the ring from her finger, and saw that the eyes of the slave-girl flickered hungrily. "Give me five minutes of talk with him, and this ring is thine! You can arrange it. Who would know? A gold-piece or two from that girdle of thine, and the guards will bring him."

The slave-girl rose lithely. "By Allah, I will risk my neck for a jewel like that! Wait and see, lady. Perhaps it can be arranged."

WHEN THE girl had vanished, Sefid rose and went to the pearl-inlaid table in one corner of the room, where she found ink and brushes and paper. She still wore her usual dress of white silk, which she had snatched up at the moment of her abduction, and the great pearl still shone upon her hand amid the jewels which Uthman al Hudr had sent to her from the spoils. Gazing meditatively at her ring, and writing her vowels with some difficulty, she composed a letter which was rather calculated to startle the recipient—although to startle him was not her intent.

> In the name of the Compassionate! To Agha Fraser, greeting. I who write am Sefid, daughter of Tahir Beg.
>
> If you are that Nazarene who was my father's friend, death is not far from you; I know many old hatreds that are living. There is no present help for us. Al Hudr is going to take us both to Penjivan, meaning to marry me and to torture you.
>
> Tahir Beg thinks I am a prisoner in Sulaimanieh, and he is fighting there; with him is your son. I think that Al Hudr means to go home and leave Shaik Nuri to the mercy of Allah. In that case, we can escape and then seek Sulaimanieh, where we shall find my father.
>
> Trust no one among these idolaters. Trust only the one who comes to you by night and loosens your bonds in the name of Tahir Beg. Allah and Ali his prophet watch over you!

Sefid read over this letter, nodded in satisfaction, and rolled it into a tiny ball which she concealed in her palm. She returned to her heap of cushions, waiting, giving no outward sign of the heart-pounding within her. If she were cool, it was of necessity. There would be time enough for weeping once fate had claimed her; until then she meant to fight!

She had no illusions about trusting the slave-girl; the black eunuchs, too, would be watching closely what passed. So, when the bolted door softly opened, she displayed no eagerness. Outside the quiet of night had fallen upon the village; fires twinkling across the ancient plain showed that a caravan was being prepared for marching at dawn.

Into Sefid's apartments came the slave-girl, followed by two of the black eunuchs, who gripped between them a prisoner.

That Fraser had not easily been captived was apparent from his torn clothes and blood-streaked face; on one cheek was the purple welt of a blow. Yet he bore himself calmly enough, and from the first glance of those steely eyes Sefid knew that here stood the father of Bob Fraser.

YAWNING INDOLENTLY, she rose to her feet and approached the prisoner. Thinking that he had been brought to be made sport of by some favorite, Fraser met her gaze with square contempt and scorn; none the less he could not keep a hint of admiration from creeping into his eyes at sight of her beauty. Laughing a little, Sefid peered into his face, then touched with languid fingers the wrists that were bound before him.

"These Englishmen are strong!" she exclaimed, and the black slaves grinned at her. "He has wrists of steel, by Allah!"

She had not mistaken her man. Fraser gave no sign that he felt the tiny ball of paper thrust against his palm, but his fingers clenched upon it.

"Do you speak Persian?" asked the girl curiously. He answered coldly.

"Yes, lady." A little wonder crept into his eyes as he gazed upon her beauty.

At this instant the door opened again and Al Hudr came into the place. From the slave-girl broke a cry of fear, but the Persian smiled and came toward them. His smile was as cruel as his glittering eyes.

"Peace be with you!" he uttered ironically. "Why did you not send to me with your request, White Pearl? I can deny you nothing, sweet one; when the month of Auril is past, after which marriage may take place according to the law of the Black Book, you shall be mistress of all Penjivan. Until then be patient, White Pearl. Do you know this Englishman?"

"I have never seen him before," said Sefid with candor. "Often I have heard my father, Tahir Beg, speak of one named Agha Fraser."

Now, at this Fraser started slightly; it was his first intimation as to the identity of the girl before him. Al Hudr smiled thinly.

"And this is the same man, little one," he said, viewing Fraser with chilled eyes. "When I have finished fighting here and have come to Penjivan with my men, this infidel shall be hung by his heels at the gate and slowly sliced asunder. I remember we did that to some of the accursed Armenians at Van, and they ceased not to curse us until the knife had reached their hearts. Let us see, Agha Fraser, if you are brave as they!"

Fraser bent upon him a scornful gaze.

"Words are cheap, Uthman," he said quietly. "Loose me and give me a sword, and I will do worse to you than I did in the past, when my slaves beat your feet into a raw mass! Dost remember that day, Persian, and how you howled under the beating?"

Al Hudr went livid, and his hand trembled upon his knife. But his face cleared again in a smile, and that smile of his was more deadly than the fury that had lighted his eyes.

"Words are cheap, as you say," he returned smoothly. "Take him to his place, you slaves, and see that he is well watched. As for you, White Pearl, go to your rest, for with the morning you must travel. I have made ready two breed camels for you, with a sling between them; it is no easy road to Penjivan, and you will have need of repose tonight."

He withdrew, beckoning the slave-girl as he went. Trembling, she followed him. When the door had closed, Sefid heard a low, shuddering cry, followed by silence. Despite his soft words, Al Hudr was taking vengeance on the girl; and presently she crept back into the apartment, blood streaking her back where a whip had bitten, and hatred in her eyes as she regarded Sefid. There was no more help to be had of this girl, Sefid knew well.

WITH THE dawn Al Hudr appeared and placed three of the great blacks in personal charge of Sefid. She was taken out to a luxurious, carpeted swinging couch, curtained and slung between two camels; everything in the apartment was swiftly bundled aboard other beasts, and Sefid found herself part of a huge booty-laden caravan moving across the wide plain of Sharizur toward the mountain walls beyond. Al Hudr, she gathered, meant to hold off the Jaf tribesmen until the booty and slaves were safe; whether he would then go to the help of Shaik Nuri or leave that young chieftain to a well-deserved fate, she did not know—but she shrewdly conjectured that the latter course would be followed.

With Sefid was the slave-girl, sullen and silent. Two of the blacks walked in front, one in the rear, hands on revolvers; there was little to be feared from the rough convoy of the caravan, however, for Sefid was marked as the property of Al Hudr, who was healthily feared by his hillmen.

The day's march was terrific, and Sefid knew that she must get away that night or never. Across the plain wound the caravan, horsemen on its flanks to guard against any Jaf rovers, and a billowing cloud of dust settled over it as it went. The air was hot, stagnant and insufferably humid, for it rained much at night, and water stood in depressions of the plain until it had evaporated; yet the dust was not stilled, but rose in tormenting clouds.

During the day Sefid discovered that Agha Fraser was in the rear of her camels, being marched along with certain slaves chosen by Al Hudr as his own. When the caravan halted for the night, it was beside a small stream, whose trees supplied firewood; rain threatened, and although the halt was only until midnight, tents were spread for the more fortunate ones. Of these was Sefid, who was treated with the usual freedom of the Kurdish women; yet she was closely watched by the blacks, one of whom was always on guard at the tent entrance.

By the time darkness fell, the evening meal had been disposed of and everyone in the camp had settled down for a few hours of exhausted repose. Inside their black goat's-hair tent Sefid waited in patience until the slave-girl curled up and slept; then, sliding from its sheath a long, thin knife she had secreted, Sefid went to the entrance. The sky was clouded; everything outside was pitch black; barely a foot distant she could see the broad back of the black slave who stood on guard.

Cautiously, Sefid extended the blade. She had thought to slay the eunuch; yet something within her revolted; not for her life or honor could she murder the man thus.

"Quiet!" she whispered as the steel pricked him. "Take off your abba and drop it; then hold your arms back this way."

A start of amazement broke from the mute, but the pricking of cold steel warned him. He loosed the long abba of camel-hair that cloaked him from head to foot against dust and heat, and it fell about his feet. Then he reached backward—and a grunt broke from him as his hands clutched upon Sefid. He whirled, and drew her to him in a great grip, striving to prison her.

That grip was his death, for between them was Sefid's hand and dagger. The mute worked his own bane, crushing Sefid suddenly to him so that the steel bit under his ribs and sucked at his life. He released her, staggered back a pace and then came to his knees.

Frightened by this chance, only dimly understanding how it had happened, Sefid snatched down at the abba and wrapped it about her, pulling the hood over her golden aureole of hair. Then, remembering that she was weaponless, she stepped to the body of the black and took from him two revolvers, with the bandolier of cartridges.

The first drops of rain were just falling. From every hand came the grumbling mutter of camels, the stamping of donkeys, the complaints of men; the deathly darkness was increased by occasional flashes of lightning. From somewhere came the mocking taunt, "Nt 'lat Shaitan! Accursed be Satan!" of some Kurd or Persian, followed by the angry response of a Yezidi and the clash of weapons.

Passing a guard unseen and unheard amid the confusion, Sefid glided among the captives who were stretched out shelterless. Among these she passed swiftly, and presently came to a silent figure a little apart from the others. This was Fraser; she recognized him by a flash of lightning and dropped down at his side.

"La allahu il'allah!" she exclaimed calmly. "My knife is gone, *agha;* but I can use my fingers on those bonds of yours. In the name of Tahir Beg!"

"Who are you?" muttered Fraser, holding out his bound hands.

Sefid only laughed softly into the folds of her abba, and pressed a revolver into his unbound hand for answer.

"Now come! We must steal horses and be off."

CHAPTER IX

"I GIVE AND TAKE AWAY; I CAUSE BOTH HAPPINESS
AND MISERY."—*REVELATION OF MELEK TAUS.*

FRASER FOLLOWED Sefid through the camp, not guessing who she was, deeming her some spy of the Jaf or Hamavand peoples. He did not greatly care; within himself Fraser was in turmoil and stress of spirit.

During his brief period of captivity he had learned much from the talk of those about him. Tahir Beg, he discovered, was far from dead; he also gained an excellent idea of the existent state of affairs as regarded Shaik Nuri and others. He knew now that Ra'sul Majid had been luring him into a trap at Sulaimanieh, and that Shaik Kadir must have recognized him again there in Samara. His awakening was terrible and complete.

Silent, he followed his guide through the murky camp, now exchanging a rain-dampened greeting in Persian with bedraggled warriors, now rebuffing the snaky heads of biting camels, ever searching here and there for horses. At last they came to a clump of these, still saddled and bridled. Here, as the girl paused, Fraser touched her arm and spoke softly.

"Do you come from the White Pearl?"

"Yes."

"Has she also escaped? If not, then—"

For reply, the girl put her face close to his and drew aside the hood of her abba, so that even in the darkness he could sense her features and the golden cloud of her hair.

"Horses, now, and away!" She caught at his arm. "The men will be sleeping close by. I will get two of the animals; you be ready to fire in case there is an alarm."

She glided away from him before he could answer, and was lost in the darkness.

Fraser waited, reflecting within himself how this wonder-girl had not only effected her own rescue but had also extricated him. He considered miserably whether she were aware of the part he had played in her past life, the influence he had exerted on all her years! No, she would know nothing of it, he decided.

Presently she came back to him.

"Two of the horses are free. We must ride, and ride hard! They will hear us; we must throw them into confusion, and hide for a little space. Then we can go on our way."

Fraser assented. She guided him to the two beasts she had separated, and was in the saddle of one at a leap. More slowly Fraser swung up. From the darkness jumped out a sharp exclamation, a curse, a cry of alarm; Fraser answered with a shot from his revolver, then sent his horse after that of Sefid, dimly visible in the darkness ahead.

Behind them lay pandemonium. Shoots rang out, shots split the night; no man knew if the caravan were attacked or if the *jinn* of the mountains were upon them. Horsemen sped through the camp, creating worse confusion; captives wailed; women shrieked; men shouted oaths and orders. Out of it all rode Fraser and Sefid, free.

They rode at a gallop, until the girl turned her horse sharply aside from the track. A jagged lightning-flash had shown her, half a mile distant, one of the mounds that marked long-forgotten palaces or towns of the Sassanid kings; and toward this she headed.

"No shelter from the rain," her voice drifted to Fraser, "but safety from any bands of horsemen. Later we can go on. Just now they will all be scouring the plain."

They found a clump of trees near the great mound and came to earth. Fraser busied himself contriving a shelter of boughs, with sorry success; for an hour they waited, and Sefid related the story of her escape. She told of Bob Fraser, sketching her own story as well.

"And now," she concluded, rising, "the alarm that we raised will have subsided, and they will have discovered my absence. We had best be off at once, before they decide to send word to Al Hudr. We shall meet no one from the caravan now, since they could not spare men upon a prolonged search after us."

"As you think best," said Fraser quietly.

MOUNTING AGAIN, they returned to the road and went forward for an hour. Fraser was very silent. He had no great hopes of ultimate escape, for the entire plain was overrun by Al Hudr's forces; indeed, upon topping a low rise they discovered torches ahead, and drew rein hastily. The rain had ceased, but the dust under foot had changed into mud, which after an hour of sunlight would be dust again.

"An encampment ahead," said Sefid calmly. "We can circle around and try to pass Halabja, and so get to Sulaimanieh."

"We had better get out of the valley before daylight," cut in Fraser. "Our best plan would be to strike direct for the closest hills and stay hidden until the Jaf tribes gather and force Al Hudr out of the whole valley."

"Very well," assented Sefid. "Forward, then! We have no time to lose."

They turned from the valley road. For a while they made slow going of it in the dark night; then by good luck they stumbled into a sheep-track that gave them freer riding. Soon they were proceeding through dank mists that reeked upward from the steaming ground; and when the mighty wall of Aorami Mountain at length loomed against the grayness of the false dawn, they were following the faint trail into the lower hills. The true dawn saw them comfortably ensconced in a deserted shepherd's hut that overlooked a secluded valley.

"Leave the horses to me," said Fraser as Sefid slipped to earth and doffed her soaked abba. "Here are dry blankets in a waterproof, strapped to my saddle. Take them into the hut and sleep. Place your wet things outside, and I'll have them dry before you waken."

Sefid obeyed with a nod, and was gone.

Fraser built himself a small fire, and before the sun rose had dried out somewhat. In the looted saddlebags he found food, with two skins of *du;* so they were assured against starvation. When he had laid out the wet garments of Sefid to dry in the sunlight, he stretched out beside the wall of the hut and was asleep at once.

I T WA S nearly noon when he wakened, to hear the bubbling laughter of the girl. She was dressed, and had made ready a meal before wakening him; the horses grazed near by, and there was no sign of any intruder in the little valley.

In the bright noonday sunlight Sefid inspected him curiously, for he was changed from the man whom she had previously seen. He looked more like his son now, and she decided that it was due to new lines of bitterness and suffering that had sprung into his face. Compassion prompted her, and she touched his cheek lightly with her lips. Fraser shrank from the touch.

"How I wish that we were standing thus beside my father's house!" she said simply. "He has told us much about you, Agha Fraser; and your son was so like you that we all seemed to know him from the beginning. See, I have a meal ready; let us eat and talk."

Fraser assented, but without joy. He perceived a hard task facing him, and he knew that he must go through with it. This girl with the eyes of gold-specked lapis, who seemed so independent, so untouched by hardships or danger, stirred him marvelously; the very beauty of her was amazing to him. He saw now that she was a different creature from the girl whom he had seen surrounded by the loot of Al Hudr and posing for Al Hudr's benefit as a languorous oriental beauty. Now she was herself, vigorous and active, her slender body animated by the spirit of the free Kurdish women, children of the mountains.

In the saddlebags he had found tobacco, and when their meal was done Fraser lighted a cigarette and smoked in silence for a space. Sefid, covertly watching his face, was frightened by the sudden stern bitterness of it. At length he turned to her and gestured toward the pearl ring upon her hand.

"You have always had that ring, Sefid?"

A flash darted into her eyes. "Yes, *agha.* Three years ago my father gave it to me, saying that it had always been kept for me; it was my mother's."

Fraser nodded. "There is writing inside it. Let me see it."

"It is strange writing," she said, puzzled, as she withdrew the ring and handed it to him. "The letters are Frankish, I think. But—how knew you of it?"

Fraser looked inside the ring. His lips tightened for an instant. Then his blue eyes smote up at her again.

"I must tell you something, Sefid," he said steadily. "We are in danger; it is right and just that you should know what only Tahir Beg and I know. Many years ago Tahir and I rode through this country and into Persia; we were friends, and I esteemed Tahir as a true man and good."

"Yes," she said, her eyes upon his. "He is all that and more, *agha.*"

"He never told you of your mother, Sefid?"

"Very little. Why?" Fraser tossed away his cigarette, facing the moment squarely.

"We rode to Sufiz, a Persian town, and sacked it," he said. "There was a French doctor there, and his family. Before we came, a mob had killed him and looted his hospital; we found his wife dying, and she confided her baby girl to my care, knowing me for one of her own race.

"I was young in those days, Sefid, and I had left my own family at home. I thought to take the child to some mission station and leave her, but Tahir fell in love with the babe's beauty and wished to keep her as his own. To me, at the time, it seemed that never would the child find a truer father than he, a more upright and noble man than Tahir; so in the end I assented, and we brought back the child with us.

"I did not realize then that I was doing wrong, but I realize it now. You have been cheated of your birthright, Sefid, brought up in a land of savages, when you should have been reared—"

"I? *I?*" The girl put a hand to her breast, staring at him. But to his astonishment, anger deepened in her eyes, and the quick flush that dyed her cheeks was passionate. "You say such things of me, Agha Fraser? How dare you! Is Tahir Beg a savage? Are the free men of the Hamavands savages? Think you I would have been reared in Frangistan, where women have no freedom of body or mind, where folk live in stone cities instead of—Oh, I am glad, glad, to be what I am! I would sooner be the daughter of Tahir Beg than empress of all Frangistan!"

Before the flashing beauty of the girl Fraser was silent. He perceived suddenly that she could not see things as he saw them, and he sighed.

"Sefid, do not mistake me. Remember that to me my own people and their customs seem best, and I have reproached myself for not having put you among them. But perhaps all is for the best. Your name is your mother's, and it is graven there inside the ring: Helene de Montfort. If you do not choose to use it, no matter. At least you know the truth, and if harm comes to me and to Tahir, you will be mistress of your own fate."

H E R O S E and walked down the valley. Sefid gazed after him, and gradually some understanding rose in her of what was stirred in the man, of how he must blame himself and why. Impulsively she darted up and ran after him, and when he turned at sound of her steps, she caught his hand, tears brimming in her lovely eyes.

"*Agha,* I am a silly girl. Allah upon you—pardon my words! I understand, and I thank you."

Fraser's face lightened in a smile, such a smile as it had not known for long. Then he stiffened suddenly; his eyes, lifting over the girl's shoulder, dilated swiftly, and became cold and piercing as steel.

"Go back!" he said in a changed voice, putting her from him. "Go back quickly. There is no time for saddling—take one of the horses and go up the valley; I will hold them off for a space, then follow."

Turning the corner of the valley below, and not a hundred yards distant, was a little group of horsemen who drew rein in astonishment at sight of the two standing there. They were no Kurds, but Persian pillagers, as their garb testified. Sefid caught her breath.

"I will wait for you—at the upper end of the valley," she exclaimed, then turned and ran for the hut.

Fraser did not drop among the boulders that strewed the little valley, but stood silent, revolver in hand, watching the raiders. There were four. They paused irresolute; then the sight of Sefid running toward the hut seemed to decide them. With a shout they plunged in their spurs and galloped straight for Fraser.

Fraser drew a breath, almost of relief, and a grim smile curled his lips. So that Sefid might escape, he was content. He knew that Bob lived, and was in good hands; and now that the elder years seemed crushing him down with forgotten sins, he was glad to face a single moment of expiation and reparation. He would stay here; it was as good an end as any!

As his revolver cracked, one of the four horsemen plunged from the saddle. The others fired in response, and did not slacken rein. They were almost upon him now. He fired again, missed, and again.

The old-fashioned revolver clicked upon a useless cartridge, misfired.

Yelling exultantly, the three horsemen swept over him. One horse struck him full, knocked him sprawling among the boulders, and he lay quiet. The three spurred on, their leader shouting madly, to where Sefid was scrambling astride one of the barebacked horses. Escape was hopeless. She turned, lifted her revolver, and fired pointblank. One of the three horsemen slumped over his crupper and died.

Before Sefid could fire again, the leader had seized her, pulled her to him, wrenched away her weapon. She looked into his brown, laughing face, and an astonished word broke from her lips.

"Jafir!"

Jafir—for it was indeed the same ill-conditioned youth who had suffered from Bob Fraser's hand and had fled from among the Hamavands to join the outlaws—laughed exultantly. Unheeding her frenzied implorations, he deftly stripped the kerchiefs from his high Kurd cap, bound her and laid her across his saddle, holding her in one arm.

Then he turned to his remaining companion, a Persian follower of Al Hudr, deliberately pistoled the unsuspecting man in the back, put spurs to his horse and spurred up the valley toward the hills at a wild gallop. To the girl who writhed impotently in his arms he paid no heed, save to grip her the more closely.

An hour passed. Among the scattered boulders Fraser sat up, then slowly came to his feet; he tried to walk, and staggered. He examined his body.

"Nothing broken, I guess," he muttered, and stared about. "Badly knocked up—bruised. Where's Sefid. Damn that revolver!"

He sank down upon a boulder, his head in his hands, realizing how he had failed, and that Sefid was gone.

In the distance the noise of hooves and jingling bits arose, but Fraser did not move; he was too broken to care for anything. A band of riders came slowly down the valley toward him, among them a white man. As their garb testified, they were of the Jaf tribe; two of them were from an eastern subtribe, wearing Persian gear. Fraser looked up as they drew nearer, and from these two brethren, who were A'in and Ma'un, broke a cry of recognition. The white man sent his horse leaping toward Fraser, and scrambled from the saddle with tears of joy upon his cheeks.

Winkler had come back again to his master.

CHAPTER X

"KNAVES, THIEVES AND TREACHERS, BY SPHERICAL PREDOMINANCE."—*KING LEAR.*

BOB FRASER, with six daredevil Hamavands behind him, was riding leisurely across the storied plain of Sharizur, toward sunset of a day which, compared to his past week of riding and fighting, had been uneventful. On the previous evening he had left Sulaimanieh, and was now within sight of Halabja; he and his six had been out twenty-four hours and were good for another forty-eight; at least, the Hamavands were, for such is Kurdish endurance.

Tahir Beg had captured a corner of Sulaimanieh, in the face of an obstinate resistance by Shaik Nuri. That the days of the Shaiks and their lawless men were done in this city there was clear proof; the whole force of the Hamavands was behind Tahir Beg, while many of the Jaf men were flocking to aid him. From these, however, Tahir Beg had found that Al Hudr was sweeping the Sharizur Valley with fire and sword; also, he discovered that Shaik Nuri expected Al Hudr to come and aid him against the Hamavands.

Had Tahir Beg dreamed that Sefid was not in the city, he would have wasted no time here. Of this, however, he was ignorant, despite conflicting tales from the prisoners he took. The one thing that was clear was that Al Hudr was expected to return and help Shaik Nuri. So, in order to get some definite information on this head, Bob Fraser and six of his men rode toward Halabja to reconnoiter.

After twenty-four hours of riding Fraser had come into the Sharizur plain, but had met only a few fugitives. He was at a loss to comprehend the situation. Most of the Persian forces were now retiring; Al Hudr and a chosen company were covering the main retreat by scouring the plain, scattering small bodies of the gathering Jaf men, and keeping Halabja convinced that the siege was maintained. Not being able to know this, Fraser was puzzled. The fugitives told him of great armies of idolaters covering the plain, but he found none.

The sun was setting when Bob Fraser led his six riders into a village which, as they came in, appeared abandoned and empty. Before the first man was out of the saddle, however, a sudden voice rang out from the house before them.

"Agha Fraser! Come quickly!"

It was the voice of Sefid; Fraser recognized it, and forced his incredulous senses to action. He was the first out of the saddle and into the house, a large one of two stories. The six Hamavands piled after him with a yell, and finding nothing below stairs, Fraser dashed to the upper floor.

And there, coming toward him, he saw Sefid.

THE WONDER of finding her thus left him speechless. He could only grasp her hands and gaze into her laughing, tear-happy eyes, while the Hamavands clustered about with exclamations of surprise and delight. Sefid was the first to find her voice.

"Jafir!" she cried with sharp recollection. "He brought me here—he was here a moment ago."

At the same instant, the sound of hooves rose from the street below. Back rushed the six riders, to see a horse disappearing down the village street, with a figure bending low in the saddle. Jafir, at first taking the party for Al Hudr's men, had soon discovered his mistake—and when Sefid called for help, Jafir had stolen away.

The Hamavand rifles cracked, but Fraser forbade pursuit. He turned wonderingly to the girl.

"To think of finding you here, safe and well!" he exclaimed, staring at Sefid as though doubting the reality of her presence. "What has happened? Where have you been?"

"With your father," she answered, laughing.

"My—my father?" For a terrible instant Fraser thought her mad.

"Yes. Then Jafir came—and brought me here. Poor Jafir knew nothing of what had taken place; he kept me bound and gagged until we reached here an hour ago, and he was foraging for something to eat when you came."

"In the name of Allah!" said one of the Kurds, laughing. "Tell us from the beginning, White Pearl!"

Betwixt laughter and happy tears Sefid outlined her story. Fraser was thunderstruck when he was informed of his father's presence in Mesopotamia, and the reasons thereof; his amazement passed into consternation at hearing of the fight in the valley.

"Can you find that place again, Sefid? If so, we shall remain here tonight, and seek in the morning for some trace of my father. You say that Al Hudr's whole force is now retiring, abandoning Shaik Nuri? Tahir Beg must have news of this! A volunteer!"

All six men leaped forward delightedly. Fraser picked one of them to bear the tidings to Tahir Beg, and within two minutes the Hamavand was clattering out of the deserted village. Not the least of the news he bore was word of Howard Z. Fraser.

Camp for the night was made in one of the houses. Sefid was confident that she could find again the valley in which Bob's father had come to grief; she had ridden in the arms of Jafir the ill-conditioned, bound and gagged, but with her eyes uncovered, and she had noted the road.

Nothing worse than anxiety had befallen her. Jafir had been forced to leave the hills, where with his captive he could neither fight nor run from the gathering Jaf tribesmen. He had been quite ignorant of her abduction by Al Hudr; and he had decided to rejoin Al Hudr and make his way to Penjivan with this gift Allah had put into his hand.

"If he had known the truth," and Sefid laughed delightedly, "he would have ridden elsewhere! So I would have told him nothing, even if I had been able; I was in less peril from Al Hudr than from him."

Weary as they all were, Fraser and his five remaining men sat up late into the night about their fire, listening avidly to the girl's story, and recounting their own tale of the fighting around Sulaimanieh. Sefid, however, said nothing about that pearl ring and what was graven thereon; nor did she touch on the secret of her parentage.

"We can let Shaik Nuri alone, now that you are safe," declared Fraser confidently. "The Jaf tribes would gladly join Tahir Beg in a stroke at Penjivan; it would be well worth having a hand in. Tomorrow night we'll be with your father, Sefid; on the way, we'll try to find some sign of my father, if you can lead us to the place where you left him."

"And if we find nothing of him?" questioned the girl gravely.

"Then we shall go on to your father, little pearl! And with the Jaf men behind us, we shall strike the devil-worshipers like a bolt from on high—eh, you wolves?"

"By Allah, that is the truth!" growled the Hamavands hungrily.

THAT NIGHT Fraser slept with devout hopes that on the morrow he would find his father not greatly harmed, for Sefid thought he had not been shot. The deliverance of the girl seemed little short of miraculous, and it was due to herself and her own ability. The deliberate and useless self-sacrifice of Howard Z. Fraser was saddening; yet Bob was sanguine in hope that his father had survived.

Awake with the false dawn, the party had breakfasted and was ready for the road by the time the true dawn appeared. Jafir had fled with one of their horses, but had left his own beast in its stead; so Sefid mounted behind Fraser. The Hamavands were jubilant; not the least cause of their joy was news that Fraser's father was in the land, for the tales of Tahir Beg's old comrade in arms were many and well known.

Leaving the empty village behind in the dawn-light, the party headed north. A quarter-mile distant was a clump of trees dotted with ruined huts, and it seemed to Fraser that he discerned a slight movement among the trees. Nothing more of the sort appeared, however, and he concluded that it had been some jackal or wild dog. None the less he sent two of the Hamavands on ahead with injunctions to keep a sharp watch for raiding-parties.

They were now following the main road that led north to Sulaimanieh, and except for a distant cloud of dust in the north, it appeared deserted. Fraser apprehended no danger save from the direction of Halabja, to the south; as he rode among the trees that fringed the road, he was laughing and talking with Sefid.

Then, sudden as a lightning stroke, from the trees came a rifle-blast that shot down the two men ahead. A burst of wild yells followed. Fraser wheeled his horse, thinking to get Sefid out of the ambuscade, but already a torrent of men was pouring over the road, with flashing of knives and wild shouts.

Fraser pistoled the nearest assailant; then his horse screamed horribly and went down, hamstrung by a Yezidi. Fraser pitched forward; as he fell, a rifle-butt in the hands of Jafir the ill-conditioned struck him at the base of the skull and swept him prostrate, perfectly conscious but absolutely paralyzed. He lay unnoticed amid the confusion and dust.

Jafir had seized upon Sefid with a wild yell, but unexpectedly other hands gripped the girl, and a long tongue of steel licked into Jafir. Above him, as he groaned and fell to sob out his life, stood Ra'sul Majid, the single topaz eye glimmering with a baleful light. The remaining three Hamavands had been pulled down. One was slain, the other two bound.

"Ho!" chuckled old Ra'sul Majid, wiping the knife that had sent Jafir to his account. "That fool had little sense, to ask *our* aid in recovering his beloved! So this is the White Pearl, eh? Al Hudr will pay us a pretty sum for this day's work, brethren! Bind the girl well."

Sefid was already bound. "Dog of an infidel!" she cried passionately. "Is it pay that you want? Then take me to Tahir Beg—"

Ra'sul Majid burst into laughter.

"Not likely!" he jeered. "Take you to Tahir and be flayed for the pains, eh? Melek Taus save me from that end! Where is that Nazarene infidel and the sacred image of—"

FOR ANSWER, Bob Fraser rose out of the dust. His revolver had been knocked afar in his fall, but he gripped Ra'sul Majid in a frenzy of rage and despair.

The one-eyed shrieked once and gripped out his knife; then Fraser's iron fingers tore it from him and buried the steel to the hilt. As the nearest of the Yezidis sprang upon him, Fraser rose from the body of Ra'sul knife in hand and met them squarely.

"*Na'lat Shaitan!* Accursed be Satan!" His voice rose at them in the taunt of Islam. "On, dogs, on!"

They came at him in a howling torrent of men, crowding and fighting each other to pull him down; for Ra'sul Majid, whose single glittering topaz eye had now closed in red dust of death, had been one of their emirs or chief men, descendants of the mythical Yezid.

Bob Fraser went down under the maddened mass, then rose again, taunting them as his knife bit deep. Those who held the prisoners were intent upon the scene; none of them observed that the dust-cloud on the road to the north had resolved itself into mounted men, fast approaching. The two Hamavand captives yelled wild encouragement to Fraser until their captors smote them into half-stunned silence.

Those nearest Fraser were too crowded to use their weapons to advantage, while those behind jammed them forward. Every stroke of Fraser's bit deep. Their knives were finding him, but without mortal hurt. The circle of men billowed in upon him again, and he went down under the mass; above the place rose a great cloud of dun dust, so that it was hard for those outside the circle to see what happened there.

Once more Fraser emerged, dusty, bleeding from many slight wounds, his taunting voice goading the Yezidis into new madness, his knife striking ever home. About him lay men dead or dying, dust-choked; among their yelling comrades he rose grim and terrible, until at last a dying Yezidi caught his ankle and he went down.

Over him they crowded, hurling themselves for a stroke at the infidel, fighting frenziedly to be at him. Yet he was not done. The mass of men upheaved in a great wave, as the water upheaves over some rock that is hidden but potent, and forth from the struggling mass came death-yells.

Quiet for an instant; then a fresh upheaval, and the scream of a man as Fraser's knife tore at his soul. After this the dust began to settle, until suddenly a wild yell of surprise and consternation burst from one of those holding the captives—and was answered by a thunder of hooves and the shouts of men. The riders from the north had come up, unobserved!

OUTNUMBERED TEN to one, the little band of a dozen Yezidis could neither fight nor flee to their horses. They huddled close, while about them swept the strangers with exultant shouts; yells of recognition arose, and from the Yezidis joyful cries. Only in Sulaimanieh is the four-hundred-year old Persian dress still worn—sleeves dragging the ground, skirts trailing in the dirt!

Yet although the Yezidis welcomed these riders as friends and allies, amazement grew among them. Midmost of the band rode Shaik Nuri, a bloody cloth about his head, and his right arm in a sling; scarce one of those who followed him was not wounded, the horses were white with lather of hard riding, and as the party drew rein, one man pitched from his saddle, dead of an old wound.

"What is going on here?" demanded Shaik Nuri, pressing to the front of things. His gaze fell upon Sefid, and he started violently. "The White Pearl! In the name of Allah, is this wizardry or truth?"

Now the Yezidis looked one at another. They knew how Al Hudr had befooled Shaik Nuri regarding the girl. Jafir was dead, and the cunning Ra'sul Majid was dead, but they were crafty men, all of them. So one of them spoke out, and with great guile lured Shaik Nuri on unto his fate.

"Who the woman is, Lord, we know not. We found her with this infidel Nazarene, and certain Hamavand riders, and caught them in an ambush." As he spoke, the man gestured toward the senseless body of Fraser. "Al Hudr is somewhere betwixt here and Halabja, sore pressed by the Jaf tribesmen."

Shaik Nuri glanced at Fraser's body, and his eyes narrowed evilly.

"That Nazarene is not dead," he said curtly. "Tie him in a saddle, one of you; I have an old tale to talk over with him. So, Sefid, you come to me at last! Peace be with you. I shall take you on to Penjivan, and you shall be consoled in my harem. Loose her, men, and guard her carefully."

Sefid looked into his eyes and shivered. She had no wish to tell this young *shaik* the truth of the situation—much better to let him take her onward with him, and trust to any chance of escape that might offer. Al Hudr would take her from Shaik Nuri, certainly; if she told the latter now how things stood, the *shaik* would evade Al Hudr and seek refuge among one of the Persian tribes, and from his eyes, she guessed that she would find in him little honor or faith or friendliness.

"Dog of Sulaimanieh, how came you here?" she demanded proudly. "I thought that the Hamavand wolves were dragging at your bloody Turkish throat!"

Nuri laughed harshly. "Proud words, girl! You are a fit mate for me. Why, I broke through your kinsmen, such of us as were left broke through, and no doubt they will be after us soon enough. Well, what matter? It is worth losing Sulaimanieh to have gained such a jewel as you! To horse, comrades; no time for resting here!"

The Yezidis dragged forth their hidden horses, and certain of them rode on ahead to find Al Hudr and to acquaint him with what had taken place.

Shaik Nuri rode forward with his band of war-broken men, little guessing that he was not riding to meet a strong ally and protector. Ever as he rode, his evil eyes dwelt upon the proud figure of Sefid, nor did he dream that before the day was over she was to be plucked from him by the mocking hand of Uthman the Persian, lord of Penjivan.

In the rear of the company rode Fraser, senseless, bound to a saddle.

CHAPTER XI

"THIS IS not so bad," reflected Uthman al Hudr with great complacency. "I lost the White Pearl and Agha Fraser, may Melek Taus curse him! But now I have gained the White Pearl again, and with her the son of Fraser—and I think I can take vengeance upon the son no less than upon the father!"

A smile grew in his dark, stern face as he gazed upon the moving cavalcade.

Free of all Jaf vengeance had escaped Al Hudr and his men—free with their booty and slaves, past the Aorami mountain wall, past that steep and precipitous defile which led into the Penjivan fastness—that defile which ten men could hold against an army—and they now were heading homeward.

Bob Fraser, riding bound among other captives—most of whom were women or girls—was glimpsing a district upon which few outsiders had ever looked. Ahead, towering into the blue sky, was the mighty rock of Penjivan; a rock of sheer scarp, a black segment of the Persian land upthrust at heaven in challenge. Here, and in the few valleys around that could be entered in only one or two places, had dwelt through ages the Persian sect whose Yezidi brethren were strewn in Mesopotamia.

From the talk of those about him, on that fast, hard flight into refuge, Fraser had learned much. The religion of the Satandevotees forbade them any dealing with the outside world; the faith of these Persian folk differed somewhat from that of their kin over the border, and among them had arisen Al Hudr, a commanding force not to be denied. He had welded them as he wished and was now their emir in rule as well as in religion.

Primitive were the habitations that nestled among the crags and hillsides, and primitive were the people who gazed upon the long columns winding through the secluded valleys. Wild mountaineers were these worshipers of Satan, yet as he came among them and passed their villages and listened to the talk

around him, Fraser was astonished more and more by the simplicity of the folk and the quaintly stark contradictions of their faith—a faith which comprised the beliefs of Islam, the Mosaic customs of the Jews, and the sacraments of Christianity.

At the doorways of all the houses that he saw, were great clusters, of crimson flowers; and when he questioned one of his guards concerning this, he found that in the month of the Yezidi new year every family of baptized devil-worshipers adorned their doorways thus as a symbol of their faith—the Black Book commanded it, said the warrior. Upon Fraser hinting that the custom might have been borrowed from the Jews, the Persian scoffed loudly and berated him for an ignorant infidel.

IN THE midmost of that caravan, his gloomy band of men around him, rode Shaik Nuri. He and his followers had sent their women-folk and choicest possessions on to Penjivan, when first the fury of Tahir Beg and the Hamavands had burst on Sulaimanieh; so that they were now forced to go thither themselves. It was a bitter pill for that proud Shaik Nuri; a most bitter pill, for now Al Hudr had taken the White Pearl from him, and on every hand the Yezidis jibed and scoffed at him— and to be the butt of such a joke is anguish to every Moslem! Yet he was helpless; against the power of Al Hudr he dared nothing.

The Yezidis, hill warriors all, thought that their leader had played a crafty and clever game. The White Pearl had been

stolen, and all the blame and brunt had fallen upon Shaik Nuri, who had lost his City and barely escaped with his life. Escaping, he had found the White Pearl and had blindly carried her on to Al Hudr—who had blandly taken her again. An excellent joke!

The great point to this jest was that in the Yezidi mythology the name of White Pearl figured largely as a symbol of the creation. Therefore it was very meet that Al Hudr should mate with her, after this month of the new year should be past; for this reason, also, great honor was paid to Sefid. As he marched with Al Hudr's personal slaves and booty, Bob Fraser watched the breed camels which bore her, on ahead; presents were showered upon her by all the folk—gifts of flowers, jewels, cloths, by those who sought her future favor with Al Hudr. And this fact gave Bob Fraser an inspiration.

Since that morning when he had departed to fetch flour, Bob Fraser had not returned to the house of Tahir Beg; he had ridden hard with the chieftain, and had been in the thick of the fighting at Sulaimanieh. Thus, he had been given no chance to deposit the brazen peacock with his own effects, for Tahir Beg carried no baggage in the field.

Wishing to keep the brazen image, which promised to have some value, Fraser had sewn it into a corner of his saddle-bags. These bags had been woven, in *kilim* fashion, by Sefid herself, and had been a present to him from the girl. Now, on the march into Penjivan, Bob Fraser had noted that in the division of the booty his horse and saddle had fallen to the lot of one of the guards who watched over Al Hudr's slaves.

Except for being stripped of his weapons, Fraser had not been robbed; at the time of his capture there had been great haste and confusion, and later on it was no doubt thought that he had been stripped by his first captors.

So, on the night before they came to Al Hudr's stronghold on the Penjivan rock, Fraser took his store of English gold from his belt, and went to this guard.

"Here, friend," he gave the man a sovereign as he spoke. "There are more of these if you will do me a certain favor—one that will advantage you also, by Allah's grace!"

"Well said, infidel! Speak!"

"When I was among the Hamavands, I knew the White Pearl well," pursued Bob Fraser. "On that horse which you ride is her own saddle, and the bags were woven by her own hand. Take them to her, and she will be much pleased with the gift. Mention my name, that she may intercede for me with Al Hudr; she will bear you in mind also, and these things may lead to some good for both of us."

"By the bird of Melek Taus, that is good news!" exclaimed the warrior eagerly. "Keep your gold, infidel; I have more plunder now than I can carry, and this news will make the fortunes of us both. Good! I will make the gift this very night."

So the man did, reporting later that Sefid had received the bags with great joy; and accounting his future assured, the warrior was only too glad to help Fraser on the march. Since the saddle-bags had thus come to Sefid, Bob Fraser was certain that her wit would see some hidden reason therein, and would find the brazen peacock. It might be of great use to her in any emergency, he knew.

As for himself, he had no hope, realizing that Al Hudr meant to vent that ancient hatred upon him. Sefid had informed him of the things that lay betwixt his father and Al Hudr, and Fraser did not doubt that the chieftain meant to take vengeance upon him for his father's actions of sixteen years previously.

O N C E O R twice he saw the two Hamavands who had been taken prisoner with him; they were slaves, and seemed to be accepting their lot with a stoical calm. Of escape there was no chance, and any hope of rescue seemed equally vain. To north, east and south the Penjivan valleys were defended by the great ramparts of the snowy peaks; the only direct entrances, from the west, were capable of being defended by small forces against any army. Here in these mountain fastnesses the Yezidis had dwelt for centuries unmolested—fierce fighters, too poor to make the effort of conquering them profitable.

Uthman al Hudr was now making them rich with plunder, bringing the world to them; and Fraser, when he saw the city of Penjivan open before him, knew that the chieftain had seized upon and made the most of the chance of a lifetime.

In ancient days some fortress of the Sassanid kings had crowned this, mighty rock, whose flat top and devious ascent made it an impregnable stronghold for the folk dwelling in the valleys roundabout. The old walls were here, repaired by Uthman, enclosing the whole surface of the hill-crest; and within the walls were buildings, new and old. Fraser gained an impression of wide streets, stout stone-built houses with scarlet flowers at their doors, fountains and running brooks beside the way. Then, before his immediate section of the caravan, opened a gate in a wall—and he was in the center and very heart of this ancient town, the citadel or palace of the old kings that was now the palace of Al Hudr the adventurer.

This, like the outer town, conveyed the idea of being new yet ancient—the walls, huge blocks of hewn stone, repaired and renewed; the decorations, the tiles, the extensive gardens, all seeming to have been done on ancient lines. Al Hudr had taken this ruined city of the kings and had restored it faithfully. Within this citadel was actually an inner city—and for this there was a reason.

Bob Fraser was kicked into one of a number of cells that lined the inner side of the wall. These cells overlooked the gardens, among which were situated other buildings; the palace, the chief local shrine at which the Yezidis worshiped, the harem or "forbidden" quarters of the women belonging to the inner garrison, and other structures. Gazing forth from his cell at this scene, Fraser soon came to an understanding of the situation here in the inner city. It was not hard to comprehend, for numbers of men were continually passing the line of cells, their talk deafening the ear. And of these men, few showed the distinctive garb of the Yezidis. Many of them wore the forbidden blue, nearly all were Persians of Kurds, as their attire testified, and most of them swore by Allah rather than by Melek Taus.

Al Hudr, the adventurer, may have been originally a Yezidi; at any rate, he had come here to Penjivan and had gathered a force of outlaws behind him for a nucleus. Around this nucleus he had gathered the Yezidi folk from their scattered valleys. Here in the inner citadel he lived with his chosen band, all of whom were of course nominal converts to the religion of Melek Taus, and from here he was extending his power in a widening arc.

It was no mean power. From the talk he heard, Fraser gathered that this stroke at the Sharizur plain was the first really extensive blow that Al Hudr had dealt. There were to be no more scattered raids, no more night-ridings in small bands. Al Hudr had now placed himself and his Yezidis in the field openly, contenders for temporal rule; into the lives of the isolated Yezidis he had brought the wide world, and for them he would carve a kingdom in the world. After this there would be no raids; there would be the march of armies!

A L L   T H A T long afternoon, as into the inner citadel poured the slaves and the loot of Al Hudr and his chosen band, the talk poured up like incense before the cells; Fraser heard much boasting about future deeds—extending a conquest over Persia was the least of the intended triumphs. Alliances, he gathered, had been already formed with many tribes around, and one of Shaik Nuri's dejected men was solemnly promised that within two months the *shaiks* would be restored to Sulaimanieh and placed at the head of all the Kurdish tribes.

"They're wild, drunk with exultation and blood!" reflected Fraser, sitting in his bare cell and watching the dusty scene from gloomy eyes. "Al Hudr has given them plunder and fighting. These Yezidis, oppressed and scattered for ages, have gathered around his tangible and visible standard with all their fanatical strength—he's an able devil, all right! I wonder where dad and Tahir Beg are, this minute?"

To this there was no answer.

With the morning, he had sight of Uthman al Hudr, who entered the inner city in triumph, passing within a hundred yards of the prison cells. The chieftain wore now a helmet and suit of chain-mail such as may still be found in Persia—more for romantic appearance than for utility—and over his shoulders was slung a huge cloak of vivid green. This, no doubt, was the reason of his nickname Al Hudr, or the Green One. Fraser never afterwards saw him without this cloak, which he appeared always to wear when in Penjivan.

Uthman's men lined the walls and the street leading into the gardens; behind the chieftain was a long procession of the Yezidi folk, headed by their priests—*pirs* and *shaiks*—clad in ceremonial garments of white linen.

The procession passed onward to the shrine—the tomb of some Yezidi saint—and away from Fraser's sight; there was not a glimpse of Sefid, and what had become of her he knew not.

In the two days that intervened, he heard more than one scrap of talk concerning her; talk which showed him that she was not in the harem but had been given a share in the palace itself—to the Yezidis, superstitious folk at best, her name and her destined marriage with Al Hudr seemed to place her on an equality with the chieftain. Al Hudr was fostering this impression. Fraser gathered that he was intensely proud of his bride-to-be and wished by all means to increase her prestige among the people he ruled.

On the third day after this, one of the Persian guards unlocked the door of Bob Fraser's cell and summoned him forth.

"Come, Nazarene! Our lord wishes speech with you."

Fraser followed his guard, not without much relief, for he had begun to think that his very existence was forgotten. Instead of being led to the palace, he was somewhat surprised when he was conducted through the gardens to a terrace that was floored with ancient marble flags, in the midst of which played a pool of water with a small fountain in its center.

By this fountain was standing Al Hudr. The latter eyed Bob Fraser keenly, then ordered the guard to withdraw. The two men were left alone.

"Peace be with you, Agha Fraser," said Al Hudr, a thin smile on his virile features. "I have not forgotten you; but in the past days I have been busy. Do you know that betwixt me and your father lies an ancient evil?"

"I have heard something of it," said Fraser quietly. In the chieftain's face he read a cruel and intolerable pride, and it came to him that he was now to suffer torture. Yet in this he erred.

"When you fell into my hands," said Al Hudr, watching him, "it seemed to me that by taking vengeance upon you I should thus allay my hatred for your father. So, indeed, I meant to do; yet now it seems to me that this would be but a sorry action, and one most unworthy of me. My quarrel is not with you, but with your father, and with him shall I settle. So on that head, Agha Fraser, fear nothing."

"I am not afraid," and Fraser smiled a little. "I *am* astonished that there should be so keen a strain of nobility in a robber chieftain like you, Uthman. If you have no quarrel with me, why do you keep me prisoner? For what purpose?"

AL HUDR'S eyes narrowed sleepily, like the eyes of a watching cat.

"Softly, infidel! I have quarrel enough," he answered. "You slew Ra'sul Majid, who was an emir of the Yezidis, and who had been traveling among the Mosul branch of our people, exhorting them to join me here. Therefore, your death is demanded by my folk, his brethren."

"That was fair fighting," said Fraser simply. Al Hudr nodded.

"So I have heard; and by Melek Taus, it seems that you are no coward! Know you where your father and Tahir Beg now are?"

"Rattling at your gates with the Jaf tribes behind them, I suppose."

"No." Al Hudr frowned. "They have disappeared, may the angels seize on them! If they were at my gates, well and good; through those, they could not break. Well, no matter. You are here, and the White Pearl is mine."

"Unless you release her unharmed, Persian," said Fraser steadily, "fate will surely find you! If you force her into your harem, I will not rest until I have your life; and although I am your prisoner and you may kill me, my father and Tahir Beg will stay upon your trail until they have pulled you down. So take warning! Let her go free, with me, and we have no further interest in your affairs; otherwise, this crime will invite your fate—"

Al Hudr laughed softly.

"Cease your prattling, child! What care I for you or your friends? Now listen to me: do you remember the image of the brazen peacock that was in the house of Tahir Beg?"

"Yes," said Bob Fraser, "it was mine."

"My man, who bore it in the flight thence, was probably killed," said Al Hudr. "That was a great loss to me, for this image was one of the seven sacred *sanjaks* or standards of our faith, and since the days of the Emir Solomon had been handed down among the Yezidis. Where that image now is, you doubtless can tell. Besides that, two only now remain, and they are in the hands of the Mosul branch of our people. I want that brazen peacock, Agha Fraser; and for it, I offer you your life."

"Ah!" said Fraser. "I am not too greatly concerned with my life just now, Al Hudr. What about the White Pearl? If you will send her back unharmed to her father, you shall have the—"

"Fool! She is here, and she stays here—better the White Pearl than a thousand of peacocks!" The eyes of Al Hudr flashed. "Let her name not again pass your lips, infidel! It is for your life, and that alone, that I bargain. Do you accept or not?"

For a bare moment, Fraser hesitated. Then he came to swift decision.

"Where it is now, I cannot say," he answered. "But I will write a note which you will send to Tahir Beg, demanding that the brazen peacock be given the messenger; when the latter brings it here, you will release me. Is that sufficient?"

Al Hudr eagerly assented.

"Agreed! When it arrives, you shall go free—the word of Uthman upon it! Until then, give me your parole—"

"Not at all," said Fraser. "If I am a captive, I am a captive."

The other shrugged his shoulders. "Very well." Turning, he clapped his hands, and a guard appeared.

"Take this man to the palace and give him the room assigned to him," said Al Hudr. "He will write a letter, which you will bring me. *Wa'l sala'm!*"

CHAPTER XII

"I HAVE MADE IT A STRICT RULE THAT EVERYONE SHALL REFRAIN FROM WORSHIPING ALL GODS."—*REVELATION OF MELEK TAUS.*

HAVING SEEN that Al Hudr's passionate eagerness to possess the brazen peacock quite overbore his crafty prudence, Fraser had not hesitated to drive the bargain. It could only afford him a temporary relief, for it could not be long until Al Hudr would know that Sefid possessed the image; however, Bob Fraser found himself released from the cage-like cell, and he was sanguine in hope that something might turn up at any moment to his advantage.

He had no idea of buying his own life with the peacock, for he knew that the image might yet prove of tremendous aid to Sefid, and he was content to leave it thus to her. The news that there seemed to be no pursuit of the Yezidis, which he speedily confirmed by talking with his guards, was a cause of greater worry to him. He had hoped desperately—even as he knew Sefid must be hoping—that Tahir Beg would come hammering at the Penjivan valleys with all the Hamavands and the Jaf tribes following him. Also, he had hoped that his father would be with the great Kurd, for he believed his father to be still alive.

Was Tahir Beg, then, dead? Had pursuit been abandoned? It seemed incredible; yet the dwellers in the valleys below the Penjivan rock were on guard, and had seen no sign of any foes. The Kurds had attempted no pursuit of the victorious raiders.

The racial hatred between Kurd and Yezidi, a hatred centuries old, seemed stunned into quiescence.

Bob Fraser found no great beauty of architecture in the palace through which he was conducted; it was built massively of beams fetched from the mountain slopes, but the old stone-flagged floors showed that it had been reared upon some ancient site. If it was not elegant, however, it was extremely luxurious, and the rich rugs of Shafizur now carpeted its floors and added to its beauty. The palace was built about one huge central hall, which he rightly judged to be used by Al Hudr on state occasions.

Fraser was conducted to rooms in the rear of the palace, which he was informed were his. These, he found, were part of an enclosed area, which included a portion of the gardens, and which were continually under guard—either of black slaves, or of Persian mercenaries. When he reached his destination, writing materials were brought him, and he wrote out a letter to Tahir Beg as agreed upon, which his guard took over and presumably delivered to Al Hudr for forwarding.

This finished, Fraser indulged in the luxury of a bath, was wined and dined by a slave who had been appointed to wait upon him, and presently, feeling more contented with his lot, lighted his pipe and sauntered forth into the gardens.

"It's a gilded prison, all right," he reflected, "but it might be a heap worse. Those cages along the wall, for instance—ugh! For the present there's no great danger; Sefid is safe until the month is over, and that will be another three weeks. In the meantime, if Al Hudr does not discover that she has the peacock, I can hope for something to turn up. Escape may not be so hopeless—"

HE WAS thinking thus, when, turning a bend in the path that wound through this prisoned portion of the gardens, he came plump upon Shaik Nuri, who was standing there gazing at the ground in an attitude of despondent melancholy. The bandage was gone from his head, but his arm still lay in its sling. Gone, too, were the numerous weapons that had formerly adorned his person. That he, also, was a prisoner, was not hard to guess.

Shaik Nuri lifted his head and gazed at Fraser, who had halted. To his surprise, Bob Fraser found in those sensual and cruel features no blaze of animosity or hatred; only despair was stamped in them—it came to him swiftly that this young *shaik* was a broken man. For a long moment the two gazed steadily at each other.

"You are Agha Farizur," said the *shaik* dully. A gleam stirred in his eyes. "Ah! Would that I had fallen fighting beneath the Hamavand bullets, ere I had been snared in the nets of this accursed worshiper of Shaitan! Would that I had slain you in the courtyard there at Erbil, or been slain, ere I had listened to the lying promises of this Persian infidel!"

Despite the evil soul of the young *shaik*, despite that it was Shaik Nuri who was primarily responsible for all that had happened to himself and to Sefid through sending Al Hudr to steal the girl and the brazen peacock, Fraser could not but feel a twinge of pity as he looked at the broken chieftain. This free lord of the hills had been ensnared in the gins of a more subtle and powerful man, and had been ruthlessly cast aside.

"You are a prisoner, then?" said Fraser. "I thought you were allied with Al Hudr—"

For the first time a flash of hatred lighted the despondent features.

"What is honor to an infidel?" broke out Nuri bitterly. "Because I desired the White Pearl, whom he took from me, this unspeakable dog has kept me prisoned, and has scattered my men among his dog-brethren; weak as I had become, he feared me! May the tomb of his father be broken into by jackals! And you, Nazarene, you are a prisoner likewise?"

"Yes," said Bob Fraser with a shrug. "I know now, Shaik Nuri, why you wanted that brazen peacock, in the caravansary at Erbil. You recognized it as the god of these infidels?"

The other nodded gloomily and dismissed the subject, as of no importance.

"I shall never see Sulaimanieh again, or the wide plain of Sharizur, or the fertile Azmir hills!" There was no whine to the young chieftain's voice, only a note of plaintive mourning, as of one who sees his own fate very clearly and shuns it not. "And you will sit in my place, my uncle Kadir—you, the wily old fox of our family, supported by the rifles of the Englishmen! Truly said the poet Palangani: 'I see in the white beauty of women the ruin of princes and the pallor of death, and in their red lips the flaming of cities.'"

FRASER FOREBORE to remind the other that it was not the beauty of Sefid which had led him to this strait, but his own unbridled passions.

"In the name of Allah, the Compassionate, cease your lamentations!" exclaimed Fraser impatiently. "You are in no danger, *shaik*—"

The other smiled—an indescribable smile pregnant with hidden things.

"You know little of this Al Hudr, oh Nazarene! He fears me and he hates me, therefore has he condemned me to death within eight days."

"To death!" exclaimed Fraser with some incredulity. "While there are a hundred of your men here—"

The other made a gesture that did not lack pride.

"What are a hundred warriors among his hundreds? They will not see me again, for unless I abandon the true God and proclaim belief in this accursed Melek Taus, he has sworn to slay me. To win his faith a *shaik* of Sulaimanieh would be good fortune in his hand, eh? But never will I spit upon the faith of my fathers, as they would have me; never will I deny Allah and turn to the worship of Shaitan the accursed! Look to your own case, Nazarene, for I think that he will give you the same choice ere long."

Shaik Nuri abruptly turned away and disappeared among the enclosed gardens.

Reflecting often on this meeting during the days that followed, Fraser concluded that only the existence of the brazen peacock had saved him from this same choice. There had been naught to save Shaik Nuri, who had fallen horribly into the pit of his own digging. After egregiously tricking his ally, after leaving him to the mercy of Tahir Beg, after taking out of his very hand the White Pearl, the lord of Penjivan was too crafty to free so potential a foe. Yet, could he exhibit a man of this rank and fame as a convert to Melek Taus, he might be well content. It was not for nothing, however, that the Shaiks of Sulaimanieh were notorious for their bigoted and fanatical adherence to Islam, and Fraser knew that this young chieftain would never apostatize.

Through the following days, Fraser was not allowed to leave his apartment or the portion of the gardens allotted to him. Shaik Nuri did not again appear, nor did he see anyone with the exception of the two guards who remained in his rooms day and night. These, who were changed thrice daily, were members of Al Hudr's personal following; they displayed no animosity toward Fraser, but treated him much as one of themselves, whiling the time away with song and story.

Nothing had been heard of Tahir Beg or the Jaf tribes, and they taunted Bob Fraser good-humoredly that his friends had left him with the White Pearl to the mercy of Al Hudr, into whose territory they dared not follow. This seemed true enough, and worried him greatly. The most probable explanation was that his father and Tahir Beg were both dead.

UPON THE eighth evening after his meeting with Shaik Nuri, he was abruptly summoned forth by his guards, who fastened golden fetters upon his wrists and led him out into the audience hall. Here he found a great company assembled, including Al Hudr's mercenaries and the chief men of the Yezidis. Upon a dais at the upper end of the hall whither he was conducted by his guards, sat Uthman in person; and beside him, couched amid gorgeous silken carpets, was Sefid.

For a moment the eyes of Sefid and Fraser met. In that brief meeting, Fraser read that she had come to no hurt; he smiled slightly, and she answered the smile with a very slight gesture that brought sudden hope into his heart. Then he turned—and saw Shaik Nuri standing between two guards, facing Al Hudr.

"Do you still prefer Islam to the worship of Melek Taus?" demanded the chieftain, who was noted among his warriors for not wasting words.

"There is but one God, and Mohammed is the prophet of God!" intoned Shaik Nuri proudly. "Accursed be Shaitan!"

A growl rippled and eddied through the ranks of the Yezidis, but with a leap Al Hudr sprang to his feet and drew his curved scimetar—a blade that shimmered with jewels in the light of the lamps overhead. And when they saw this, from all his men went up a long howl of delight.

"Loose him, and give him the best blade among you!" cried Al Hudr, throwing off his long green cloak. "Now summon Allah to your aid, infidel, for you will have need of him! Stay—since your right arm is useless, mine shall also be tied. Here, slave!"

Summoning the nearest slave, Al Hudr had his own right arm tied about his waist. At this touch of romantic chivalry the watching crowd howled anew; but Fraser, noting how Al Hudr balanced the scimetar in his left hand, guessed that the chieftain could use either arm with equal skill.

Shaik Nuri did not shrink from the measuring of swords. Standing forth with the blade that had been given him, he lifted the steel and cried aloud:

"Allah! Allahu akhbar, the Compassionate! Great is God, the Merciful!"

A thin smile curved the cruel lips of Al Hudr.

"By the hidden name of Melek Taus—*Azazil!*" he shouted, and leaped forward.

The two blades met in midair—met and clashed, clashed again. The young *shaik* seemed transmuted by the touch of a weapon; he flung himself upon Al Hudr in a passionate fury, attacking with fire, an *elan,* that drew roars of admiration from the crowd. For an instant it seemed that he would bear down the older man by the sheer frenzy of his onrush. Al Hudr gave never a stroke back, but devoted himself to upbuilding his flaming blade into a wall impenetrable.

Then suddenly, Al Hudr's glittering steel licked out like a flash of light. So swift, so sudden and terrible was the blow that few saw it. But the chieftain leaped backward, and his voice pealed up in a shrill yell of mockery.

"Ho, infidel! Where is your Allah now?"

Shaik Nuri stood motionless an instant—then a great sigh seemed to burst from him, and he collapsed in a red heap. With its single blow, that razor-edged steel had shorn into his life and had bitten him half asunder.

A W I L D roar of voices filled the huge hall—a roar of wolfish applause, a roar of mad acclaim for the greatest and most terrible swordsman of them all! None of the Sulaimanieh men were present, apparently; indeed, Fraser later learned that ten of them had been put to death that morning, and that under this example the others had consented to embrace Melek Taus; but they were not brought to see the death of Shaik Nuri, for Al Hudr was by no means desirous of goading his mercenaries into vengeance and bloodfeuds.

Before the uproar had quieted down, and while Al Hudr was cleansing his weapon upon a cloth offered by a slave, there came a surge and wave of the bodies filling the hall. Through the crowd broke an officer, who flung himself toward Al Hudr with a shout. The chieftain roared at the crowd for quiet, and as a curious hush fell, the words of the officer came clearly to Fraser.

"Lord, a Nazarene, alone and unarmed, has been sent on from the lower valleys and has been brought through the outer city to our gates."

"A Nazarene? A prisoner?"

"Not so, lord. He has come of his own will. According to his tale, he is the slave and servant of Agha Farizur, and has come hither to serve him in his captivity."

Fraser listened, startled and incredulous. It occurred to him that Tahir Beg must have sent someone—yet that were impossible, if this arrival was a Nazarene!

Al Hudr glanced at his captive, and all eyes followed his. He frowned, then a thin smile curved his lips.

"Bring the man here," he said, "but first search him well. Who can this be, Agha Fraser? When we were in the country of the Hamavands, you had no slave."

"Who it is I know not," answered Fraser, helpless.

Down the length of the hall a lane was opened, and presently everyone craned forward eagerly, for Christians were not seen every day in Penjivan—unless under compulsion. No less eager than the rest, Bob Fraser rose on his toes. When he saw the man who was striding up the hall amid guards, a low word of astonishment broke from him. Instantly, Al Hudr was at his side.

"You know this infidel?" demanded the Persian softly.

Fraser nodded, unbelieving his own senses. "He—he has served me all my life, and my father." He lifted his voice suddenly. "Winkler! Is that really you?"

WINKLER, FOR it was none other, halted and stared around. Before him was the red mass that had been Shaik Nuri, and he whitened perceptibly. Then his gaze fell upon the figure of Fraser, and a glad cry burst from him.

"Mr. Robert! Tell these heathen that it's all right, sir—"

Eagerly, Fraser turned to Al Hudr and spoke in Persian.

"This man speaks the truth, Uthman! How he came here I know not, unless he came to this land with my father. Send him away again, I pray you, and do him no hurt—"

Al Hudr merely made an impatient gesture and stepped forward toward Winkler, who met him with a blank stare. The chieftain smiled slowly, and spoke in Kurdish.

"Whom seek you here, Nazarene?"

Fraser was even more surprised when he heard Winkler break into slow and difficult Kurdish, yet manage to make himself understood. Winkler told a plain and unvarnished tale—how he had been with Tahir Beg and Howard Z. Fraser when word came to them that Sefid and Bob had been taken prisoner; how pursuit beyond the vale of Sharizur had been futile; how he had set out with certain companions, who had later deserted him, and how he had made his way to Penjivan in the face of many difficulties in order to serve his master. It was a long tale and not quickly told.

To those who heard it, this quixotic fidelity of servant to master was not only perfectly understandable, but it was thoroughly admirable. Obviously, Winkler was frightened; and it was equally obvious that he intended to do his duty at all costs. Al Hudr questioned him regarding the movements of Tahir Beg, but Winkler knew only that he had placed Howard Z. Fraser in safe hands and had then set forth to find Bob. So transparent was his devotion that Al Hudr could not but believe his tale. To eastern minds, here was the perfect servant.

"Let it be as you wish," said the chieftain with a shrug. "You shall remain with Agha Fraser and serve him; his fate shall be your fate, and his luck your luck."

"So be it," answered Winkler, quite unruffled by the implied threat.

"If I had such slaves as this infidel Nazarene," quoth Al Hudr, gazing fiercely about the hall, "Melek Taus would be lord of Persia and Rumistan itself! Take Agha Fraser to his quarters, and send the servant with him."

CHAPTER XIII

"A SERVANT IS TO CALL THE PEOPLE, SAYING, IT IS THE CALL
OF THE PROPHET TO A FEAST."—*THE BOOK AL JILWAH.*

RELIEVED OF his golden fetters, Bob Fraser was returned to his own quarters. As though in a dream, he shook hands with Winkler; for a moment, words were beyond him.

"Good heavens, Winkler!" he exclaimed at last. "It doesn't seem possible that you're here, in the flesh! Man, it's like a piece out of the Arabian Nights—to think of you coming all through these hills by yourself—"

"But I didn't, sir," broke in Winkler, smiling.

"You didn't? Why, you just told them you did—that was what made the big hit with Al Hudr—the faithful-servant stuff and all that—"

"Yes, sir." Winkler permitted himself a grin. Much of the old formality of Winkler had vanished; adventuring had largely effaced his dignified placidity.

"Your father and Tahir Beg felt convinced that this was the story to tell, Mr. Robert. They brought me as far as the first Penjivan valley—"

"They brought you?" repeated Fraser, staring at him in astonishment. "Then—why, you old rascal! Was that story of yours all a pack of lies?"

"Just about, sir. You see, we knew that you were here, and Miss Sefid too, so it was necessary that you be reached in some way. When I suggested that I come openly, Tahir Beg was delighted; he seemed to think that these heathen would consider it quite the thing to do, just as they did. So I came. But— the things I've seen, Mr. Robert! That dead man in the hall—and to imagine that these heathen actually worship Satan, sir—"

"Never mind all that; Winkler, you're a genius—a hero! Coming here to this place by yourself, in a perfectly calm assurance—"

"I beg your pardon, sir, but it was nothing of the sort," put in Winkler. "I was scared out of my skin all the time, I assure you!"

"Damned if you showed it, then!" roared Fraser delightedly, clapping him on the back. "Bully for you! Say, what does it all mean, anyhow? Where's dad all this time? Why hasn't Tahir Beg done a thing to rescue his daughter?"

Winkler glanced around cautiously. One of the guards was at the outer door, watching them, but he had no knowledge of the English speech.

"It's like this, sir," answered Winkler, lowering his voice. "Your father had been hurt—nothing serious, but some contusions—"

"Yes, Sefid told me about that. Go on!"

"And most fortunately, I happened to meet him and brought him to Tahir Beg—"

"You? Were you knocking around on private adventures of your own?"

WINKLER LOOKED a trifle agitated. "Well, sir, I'll come to that later. It's more important just now to tell you what's what. We met Tahir Beg and then found that to pursue this Al Hudr directly would gain very little. Tahir Beg and your father met the leaders of the Jaf tribes, who were most happy to go into partnership with them, so to speak, against these heathen, sir.

"They worked out a scheme, by which most of the Jaf troops were to take their time and then to attack the lower Penjivan valleys at a given day. To break through those valleys was impossible, according to the best accounts; so your father took charge of things there, while Tahir Beg with a few hundred picked men set off to circle around through the mountains. He had guides who could bring him on the Penjivan country from the rear, where no attack was thought possible because of the mountains—and he'll break out suddenly close to this city, sir. This will so alarm the lower valleys that your father may break in there, and while they're doing that we are to set fire to the city here—"

"Whoa!" exclaimed Fraser, laughing. "Look here, Winkler—do you still read those dime novels you used to devour in the old days?"

"Eh? Why, yes, sir—"

"Well, you're making yourself into a regular bloodthirsty old pirate chief, aren't you! We've no matches, but that doesn't matter; we can kill a few dozen of the best fighters in Kurdistan, and set fire to the outer city, and maybe knock out Al Hudr as we go along—huh? Winkler, I'm surprised at you!"

"Well, sir, I'm only going by what your father and Tahir Beg said!" answered Winkler doggedly. "According to them, Mr. Robert, there would be no chance whatever in a straight attack. The only hope was to attack unexpectedly, land a big surprise when Tahir Beg got in from the rear, and then put over the finishing blow by making them think that enemies were in the very city itself. They're depending on us to do it, sir."

Fraser sobered. "All right, Winkler; we'll not fail 'em. I don't know just what we can do, but we'll see. When is this attack to take place?"

"Whenever Tahir Beg can get through the mountains, sir. He left camp a week ago—how long it will be, I can't say."

Fraser whistled. "Well, it's a gay life! Never mind. Tell me about dad!"

Until late that night the two sat up talking, and for the first time Fraser heard of how and why his father had come to Kurdistan, and of all that had happened since his coming. In return, he was able to give a coherent understanding of things to Winkler, who was very hazy regarding the Yezidis and all that had happened. Winkler, in fact, had been under the impression that he had come into a land of wild maniacs; and the barbaric splendor of Al Hudr had quite dazzled him.

UPON THE following day, Al Hudr himself paid a brief visit to Fraser's quarters, evidently to assure himself that Winkler's story was true; the chieftain was in affable mood and paid more attention to Winkler, with whom he seemed delighted, than to Fraser. To the latter he merely said that nothing had been heard from the messengers as yet.

"You've made a hit with the chief," chuckled Fraser, when their visitor had departed. "Tahir Beg had a wise hunch, all right, when he said that the faithful-servant business would go over strong. Stick to it, old boy! Hello, who's this?"

Their guards had been changed during the visit of Al Hudr. Now that the chieftain had departed, one of the warriors promptly settled down against the door and went to sleep; the other, however, approached Fraser and Winkler. He was a total stranger.

"I have a message for you, Agha Fraser. You do not remember me, of course?"

"No," said Fraser, regarding him sharply.

"I was one of Shaik Nuri's men—it was I who guarded you there upon the road, when we captured you."

"Oh! Then you are one of the apostates—"

The man flushed darkly. "Peace, *agha,* in the name of Allah!" he said, his voice thick. "We are brought to shame, all of us; our life is become as bitterness, and we live but to put a knife into this accursed infidel Al Hudr and send him unto hell. I would have done it now, except that I had a message for you—and the slaying would have meant your death also."

"What is your message?" asked Fraser coldly, not quite believing the man.

"This, *agha*. It was given to me by another of our comrades. What it is, I know not."

From an inner pocket of his Kurdish vest the guard produced a folded paper. Fraser took it and went to a window. He opened the paper and found it to be a letter in Persian:

> In the name of God, the Compassionate! Greeting to Agha Fraser from the White Pearl.
>
> Those two Hamavand men who were captured with us, have been given me as slaves. They are bold men, and are in touch with the men of Sulaimanieh. Also, I received the brazen peacock and shall use it at the feast tomorrow night, at which you are to be present. Al Hudr has promised to admit you as a guest.
>
> Leave all to me. We shall win or lose everything. When I stand up, that is the signal; join me swiftly and do not hesitate to obey me.

Fraser stared at the writing in joyful amazement. It was the first he had heard from Sefid since their capture; the first intimation he had had that she was alive and well. He turned and called Winkler to him, and translated the writing.

"There's a woman for you, Winkler!" he exclaimed. "Instead of being overcome by her position, she has gone to work and means to do something! If I had half her spirit—"

Winkler gave him a shrewd glance, then smiled faintly.

"Do you think, sir, that what she means to do can interfere with Tahir Beg's plans?"

"I can't tell, of course; but I can't see how. Perhaps she has found some means of escape—it's evident that she and the two Hamavand men have gone to work on those fellows from Sulaimanieh. Perhaps this guard of ours knows what's up. If he could get a note to her, telling about the outside situation—"

Fraser beckoned the guard, who joined them at once.

"This letter is from her who is called the White Pearl," he said quietly. "Can you place an answer in her hands?"

"Impossible, *agha*," said the other promptly. "I know not whom to trust, nor how to get the letter to her. Most of our comrades have sworn to slay Al Hudr, but some of them have been won over by bribes of women and gold, so that it were folly to trust them."

"What is intended tomorrow night at the feast?"

THE KURD shook his head. "Agha, I know not. That there is to be a feast, I knew; and many of us have received word to hold ourselves ready to act at that time. What is intended, however, has not come to us. Nor do we know whom to trust."

"Very well." Fraser reluctantly abandoned the hope of getting any word to Sefid. It would be too apt to frustrate all her own plans if discovered. He swiftly determined to trust this Kurd fully.

"I can tell you this—that certain of your kinsmen, the Jafs, are waiting to drop upon the city from the rear and attack. If there is any fighting tomorrow night, set fire to the palace and to all other buildings you or your comrades can reach. You understand?"

A flash of fierce joy gleamed in the features of the man.

"Unto Allah be glory!" he answered fervently. "I understand, *agha*. It shall be done! Now be careful—that dog yonder is stirring, and I do not think they trust me too well—"

The Kurd hastily returned to the side of his comrade and flung himself down as though lazily watching the prisoners.

"I beg your pardon, sir," said Winkler uneasily, "but on thinking over this affair, I am not so sure that I like it. I'm afraid Miss Sefid has determined to do something desperate. Now, if you could make her wait until Tahir Beg comes—"

Fraser turned and put both hands on Winkler's shoulders, meeting the man's eyes squarely.

"My dear Winkler," he said, "Tahir Beg may never come; how on earth he can get around and through those mountains, which are inhabited by wild folk friendly to Al Hudr, without giving any warning, is more than I can see. Perhaps he can do it. More likely, he can't!

"We're in a precarious situation here, apt to be slaughtered at any moment. But Sefid is in far greater peril than we—and she has more brains than I have. To interfere with anything she has planned, would be folly."

"But, Mr. Robert, what can she have planned?" persisted the puzzled Winkler. "Escape—"

"I don't know and I don't care," broke in Fraser, laughing. "We're at the end of our rope, Winkler; any day those messengers may return with news that they can't find Tahir Beg—which means that Al Hudr would string me up gladly. The chances are they've been bagged by my father and the Jafs, and when the Yezidis find that the messengers are slain, Al Hudr is going to give me a bath in boiling oil or some such pleasantry. Now, if Sefid has framed up something, we'll swing in with her and help turn the trick, that's all! So no more growling, old friend—tomorrow night will show!"

"Very well, sir," said Winkler, stifling a sigh. "May I ask, sir, whether this Miss Sefid wears trousers, like most of these women?"

"She does, Winkler—in a perfectly adorable fashion! And, old man, we're going to be married!"

WINKLER GULPED. Then: "Does she—er—know it yet, sir?"

Fraser grinned delightedly. "Winkler, you're all right! No, she doesn't suspect it yet. What d'you think dad will say when I tell him?"

"I will venture a guess, sir, after I have seen the lady. I regret that I was too much stirred by emotion when I arrived to notice anything—"

"Aren't you congratulating me?"

Winkler gazed reflectively at him for a moment. "No, sir; you must remember that I have not yet seen her—and I believe she is a heathen, sir—"

Fraser flushed, then broke into laughter. "Confound you! I always knew you had enough backbone to serve a camel, old sport! Well, you take a good look at her tomorrow night, and heathen or not, if you don't congratulate me I'll miss my guess! Besides, I'll let you try your hand at converting her before we're married."

A faint smile broke Winkler's impassivity.

"Thank you, Mr. Robert—but I'd rather not try anything of the sort. If I may say so, sir, I think the whole affair is decidedly in bad taste."

With this dry pronouncement, Winkler departed into the adjoining chamber for a bath. Fraser gazed after him, half frowning, a trifle startled by the attitude of his companion. It was undeniably true that Sefid *was* an adherent of Islam—

"Confound it, what do I care?" muttered Fraser. "If she were the queen of China I'd still think her the most glorious woman living! And there'll be some way out of it all—there's sure to be! Just at present the chances are that we'll never live long enough to talk of marrying, so why bother trouble now? But what the devil did he mean was in bad taste—talking about Sefid, or my meaning to marry her? You're a deep one, all right! I'll bet dad is missing you a whole lot right now."

With the following day, one of the giant black eunuchs called on Fraser with word that his attendance at a banquet that evening was ordered by Al Hudr, and that if he desired silk robes for the occasion they would be furnished. Fraser refused, having no mind to part with his soiled and tattered uniform—the last link left to him with the outer world.

The day dragged. He saw no more of his friend the Sulaimanian; from the Persians who guarded him he found that Al Hudr was giving the feast that evening in honor of the White Pearl. Certain fast days were provided by the Yezidi faith, but as a rule this month of the new year was celebrated with song and feast; there was little that was gloomy in their religion.

Neither Fraser nor Winkler had a weapon of any description. They were entirely ignorant of the plan Sefid had in mind, but Fraser knew the girl well enough to impress upon Winkler the necessity of instant obedience.

"We'll have to join her the instant she gives us the signal by standing up," he said, "and then we'll have to waste no time talking. Whatever she says to do, we must do! I imagine she does not know of your presence yet."

"You don't think she will actually start a row, sir?"

"If she does, we're all done for, as far as I can see," admitted Fraser. "But, if she does, then grab anything handy and hit everyone in sight! There's no telling what that girl will have the nerve to spring, and I mean to back her up to the limit. According to all I can screw out of the guards, she's been laying low and fooling Al Hudr into thinking that she's friendly and complaisant to his wishes; and if so, I imagine she'll have a big surprise in store for him! She has brains, Winkler!"

"So I have understood, sir," murmured Winkler drily.

CHAPTER XIV

"WATCH WELL IF YE CAN READ THE HEART OF A WOMAN; FOR
THERE IS NO GUILE LIKE UNTO HER GUILE."—AL BARANI.

WELL MIGHT Uthman al Hudr feel pride in himself and his achievements, as he stood in his audience hall that night and welcomed his guests. Down the length of the hall were set long tables, laden with viands which were accounted choice for Penjivan, and with wines which the Yezidi religion did not forbid. From many sources had come the dishes of gold and copper, bronze and brass and silver, even the china, which covered the tables; from the same sources had come the rich carpets underfoot, the rare Gigim and Turkoman broideries along the walls, the clusters of ancient arms and armor that upbore the lights.

At the head of the tables was the peacock throne, or rather couch, that had been fashioned for Sefid. Not for Al Hudr had this been done; regal chieftain though he was, he and his men partook of the rough equality of the mountain folk, and he made no pretense to rule by any grace other than the strength of his own arm—which was quite sufficient. For Sefid, however, he had provided his best; it was a rather crude representation of a peacock facing the tables, the body serving as cushioned seat, the tail outspread above and behind. It was symbolic of Melek Taus, of course, as Sefid's name was to the Yezidis a symbol of creation, and awed murmurs came from the Yezidi leaders who arrived in the hall.

Al Hudr had emptied all his coffers to hang that barbaric seat with jewels, until the thing glittered and glimmered with radiant fires; and he had done so gladly. Never had it occurred to him to ask Sefid's opinion in the matter of the marriage. To him, as to all the Yezidis, he had captured her—and therefore she was his.

Sefid herself had done much to encourage this impression. Knowing how futile were any reluctance or refusal, she had assumed a passive role, ever greeting Al Hudr friendly wise and allowing him in his overweening pride and arrogance to draw his own conclusions. She was a woman, and she had only woman's weapons with which to fight; therefore, she used them relentlessly and terribly.

When she came through the doorway behind the peacock, and stepped forward, a mighty shout of acclaim arose from the crowded hall, and Al Hudr joined in it as he came forward to welcome her and lead her to her seat. She was clad plainly and simply in white, the golden shimmering crown of her hair casting a glory about her face; from the passionate eagerness of Al Hudr she shrank a trifle, then placed her hand in his and smiled. At sight of the peacock throne, her eyes widened amazedly. Al Hudr looked into those eyes of deepest blue, speckled like richest lazuli with gold, and laughed in delight of her. As though to set off her beauty by contrast with his own garb, he wore only his usual Persian chain mail beneath his mantle.

"Welcome to the White Pearl!" he said gravely. "See, Melek Taus awaits his beloved! I shall sit at your feet and worship, beauteous one—"

"No," she broke in, standing beside the peacock to survey the place. "No, Al Hudr! Sit yonder at the tables, facing me, so that I may see you!"

AT THIS arose great laughter, for the speech was taken to be the naïve words of a girl drunk with proud love of her future lord. In this sense, too, Al Hudr understood her; and seeing her confusion before all the folk, he broke into soft laughter and assented.

"As you wish, White Pearl! Name then my seat, and I shall rejoice in your eyes."

Sefid indicated a seat that was some distance away, but facing her—a seat from which Al Hudr could not easily come to the peacock throne, by reason of the tables between. To this seat the chieftain went, and gaily lifted a winecup toward her, and drank.

Thus the feast began, while there was much music of Yezidi timbrels and Kurdish flutes, and wine ran freely.

Sefid, sitting upon her peacock throne and gazing across the crowded hall, was very pale with realization of what was to happen here by her plotting. The great mass of folk were Yezidis, both men and women; all of Al Hudr's Persian and Kurdish warriors were here also, save those watching at the outer gates and walls, and many of their wives likewise. Behind the feasters were slaves—huge black men, dumb eunuchs, many girls, dancers and wine servers, and others. At either side of the peacock throne stood the two Hamavand men, who served Sefid as slaves; and this night their eyes were glittering with strange fires.

Among the throng, too, were many of Al Hudr's men whose eyes were fastened upon Sefid with the same glittering intensity—men who had once worn the long garments of Sulaimanieh, men who had served the dead Shaik Nuri, and would serve him still. Sefid smiled as she met their eyes, and there was something terrible in her smile—but her face softened when she saw Bob Fraser, at one of the nearer tables, watching her. When she smiled at him, her eyes were alight with a merry greeting. Then she saw the man who stood behind and served him.

She turned to one of her faithful Hamavand men, frowning.

"Who is that man serving Agha Fraser? Is he not a Naza-rene? Find out for me."

The Hamavand called one of the blacks who was passing, and Sefid questioned the slave. She found what was known about Winkler, and nodded. That Winkler had come as a mes-senger from her father or from Fraser's father, she did not doubt.

"Good!" she said in Kurdish to the Hamavands. "That will mean another helper—good! Tahir Beg has had some hand in his presence here, brethren!"

The two Hamavands looked at each other, and laughed fiercely.

For this night of gaiety Al Hudr had called into play all his resources, and as the wine flowed more freely the abandon of the entertainment was increased. The numbers of the musicians were swelled; party after party of dancing girls filled the side courts or threaded their way among the tables—now luring the feasters with seductive, half-clad dances of the harem, now masked and costumed in grotesque barbarity. Between the dances, men fought with scimetar or knife; fought in wild ex-hibitions of swordsmanship that brought the wine-maddened feasters to their feet in frenzied acclamations.

PRESENTLY ONE of the Hamavands leaned toward Sefid.

"It is time, White Pearl, it is time! The wine is in men's heads by now—even those Sulaimanians are drinking, may Allah requite them the shame! Presently one of them will have drunk too much—"

Sefid nodded quickly, understanding the danger. She flashed a look at Fraser, who had drunk little—a look of warning that he did not lose.

"Very well," she answered. "Go to Al Hudr and tell him to command silence, for I have something to say."

The Hamavand lingered an instant.

"Give me your permission to stay by his side, Sefid!" he breathed quickly. "Then I will have my knife through him ere—"

She flashed him an angry glance that made him straighten up.

"Have I not said that I am no assassin?" she returned heatedly. "The man is no coward, and shall not have a coward's fate! If it is the will of God that he should fall among the others, let him fall; if not, let him fight clear of them!"

"If he does that, lady, then we are lost," said the Hamavand.

"Better be lost with honor, than win by coward's blows," she retorted. "You have your own work to do; if you are unwilling to do it, then say so, and I will arrange otherwise!"

"We obey, Sefid," said the man, humbly enough, and departed.

He made his way toward Al Hudr, who, although flushed with wine, had not ceased to watch Sefid, and who guessed that a message was coming to him. He received her bidding with a nod, then came to his feet and uttered a shout that brought immediate silence. The Hamavand was already on his way back to the side of Sefid.

"Peace!" cried out Al Hudr, his voice vibrating through the hall. "The White Pearl wishes to speak. Peace, and let no man speak until she has finished!"

Silence fell, and through the hall certain men sat up straighter and watched Sefid with glittering, intent gaze.

She did not rise, however, but for a moment looked straight at Al Hudr; perhaps in that moment she was regretting all that she had planned, justifiable though it might be; perhaps the sight of this splendid barbarian, lord of the unconquered hills, stirred a womanly hesitation in her. If so, the hesitation vanished when she glanced at Fraser and met his frowning eyes.

"Children of Yezid," she said, her voice lifting clearly through the hall, "it is known to all of you that I am named the White Pearl, and you have been told that Melek Taus, whom you worship, has sent me to be the bride of your chief. Is this not so?"

A murmur of assent passed through the gathering. All eyes were fastened upon her in fascination and curious wonderment. She smiled slightly.

"Whether Melek Taus has sent me, I do not know," she went on, a sudden note of bitterness in her voice, "but if that be so, then he has no love for you. I say this, because I am not come here of my own will, and because I am not minded to marry any man—least of all, that Al Hudr yonder. Look at this, all of you! Know you what it is?"

So saying, she placed upon the peacock's head the brazen image of Melek Taus.

AN INSTANT of silence followed; then, as the thing was recognized, a low breath of awe and wonder stirred through the crowd. Al Hudr, staring at Sefid from incredulous eyes, uttered a hoarse cry which put into words the murmur of the others.

"It is Melek Taus—the sacred image—"

"Aye!" cried out Sefid, her voice ringing shrill and high as she came to her feet. "It is Melek Taus, who comes to warn you of danger and death—"

"*Na'lat Shaitan!* Accursed be Satan!" pealed forth a wild cry. In the center of the hall uprose one of the men of Sulaimanieh; his knife flamed high, and was buried in the throat of the nearest Yezidi.

Al Hudr leaped forth, but a man tripped him. Another plunged at him as he fell, striving to thrust keen steel through the Persian's chain-mail. From the doors pierced the death-shriek of a guard, and a rifle-shot banged out.

Then, when it was thought that Al Hudr was slain, wild terror rushed through the hall. None knew what had happened or what enemy had come, and as one by one men struck down the hanging lamps, all that place became a seething whirlpool of horror, in which every man fought against his neighbor and strove to escape. Nor, though presently the voice of Al Hudr rose again, did terror cease, for by now the lights were dashed away and darkness and death ruled hideously.

In vain men strove to burst through the doors; they had been barred from outside. There was fighting outside, also—certain of the Sulaimanieh men had scattered to spread fire and death in the outer city ere they themselves were slain. Within the palace every man smote out into the blindness around him, and mad panic sent the hot reek of blood drifting in air.

When he saw Sefid come leaping to her feet, Bob Fraser had sprung forward to gain her side. He had a brief glimpse of Winkler at his heels, and of the two Hamavand men striking out at those around, when he joined her. Sefid, clutching his hand, swiftly cried to follow her, and plunged into the doorway behind the peacock throne.

"None will follow yet," she panted out, as the curtains fell upon the frightful place behind them. "The Hamavands will hold the doorway—come quickly! We will meet no one this way—we must seize upon Al Hudr's tower and hold it until they come to help—"

Entirely at a loss to guess the meaning of her words, but pausing for no questions, Fraser found himself hard put to it to keep the pace she set. Swift as a deer she ran, with sure knowledge of the way, and in a moment more Fraser found that they were out of the building and in the gardens.

"There, Winkler?" he called over his shoulder.

"Right behind, sir," came the answer.

"Faster!" breathed Sefid, quickening her pace.

Fraser sprinted, marveling at her swiftness. Down the garden paths she ran, as though she knew every inch of them—so indeed she did, for this had been her study during the past days!—and behind them died out the clamor from the palace. Yet Fraser was aware of a new clamor farther away, and a murky glare that was flickering in the night. He laughed harshly as he caught up with Sefid.

"The Sulaimanians have fired the city!" he panted exultantly. "I told them—if there was trouble—to fire everything possible—"

"Good!" she answered, with a tinkle of laughter that was vibrant with excitement. "We are almost at the tower, now—there it looms ahead! There is no guard. You must get a light quickly, and find rifles—"

BEFORE THEM grew up blackly a queer structure; Fraser remembered to have seen it from his own secluded corner of the gardens, but its purpose he did not know. It was a small, perfectly round tower that now seemed to be of tremendously massive structure, rising thirty feet in air. All around it, for the space of a hundred yards or more, the garden was given over to a network of shallow basins filled with water from a fountain before the door.

Fraser was about to plunge directly at the tower, water or not, when Sefid sharply restrained him.

"Follow me! There is a path—"

She darted ahead, running between the winding curvatures of the water, pursuing some unseen pathway which led to the doorway of the tower. The door proved to be a massive affair of iron, propped open by an iron bar.

"Do not touch it!" cried the girl, as Fraser paused. "When that is removed, the door will close of itself; wait until the others join us—"

"Matches, Winkler?" demanded Fraser, coming to a halt. "I've none."

"Here are some, sir," said Winkler, the imperturbable. "Perhaps I'd better remain here, sir, to keep watch—"

"Light the lamps inside!" commanded Sefid. "Hurry!"

Fraser headed into the obscurity, struck a match, and glanced around. Directly before him he saw a large brass lamp set upon a standard. Sefid snatched it open, and he brought the match to the wick; it proved to be full of oil, for the wick burned steadily. When Sefid clashed the door of the lamp shut, Fraser saw that it was cunningly contrived to light the room around yet to leave the doorway in darkness.

"This is Al Hudr's tower," said the girl quickly. "He built it for himself as a place of refuge—or rather, rebuilt it, for it was an ancient structure before he came here. Here he keeps rifles and arms of all kinds. There is a secret passage leading to it from the palace, but I broke the lock of the secret door before I went to the feast, and he cannot use it. The pools of water are all around so that men cannot get up to the walls very quickly—"

Fraser was already getting rifles from the racks which ranged one side of the wall. With each rifle was a filled bandolier of cartridges.

"There are food and water stored in the room above," went on the girl, "and I think another passage leads off somewhere among the gardens—but I am not sure—"

Her voice failed.

Fraser turned quickly to her, thinking she was about to faint, but she shook her head and smiled slightly. She was very pale.

"No, I'm all right—it's just that—that—oh, so many men are dying this minute! But I had to do it; there was no other way—and if Al Hudr is killed I can make them obey me with this—"

She snatched the brazen peacock from her bosom, and threw it down, shuddering as she did so.

CHAPTER XV

"A HURRICANE OF FIRE AND SWORD WILL I BRING
UPON THE IDOLATERS, WHO SHALL BE SWALLOWED
UP BY THEIR OWN WICKEDNESS."—*THE KORAN.*

"THEY WANTED to assassinate him, but I would
not allow it," said Sefid more quietly. "He is too brave
a man for that—and yet, unless he dies by their steel, we are
lost! Shaik Nuri's men will cause much blood and fire this night,
and few of them will escape; few of them want to escape, after
having denied their faith! But I hope the two Hamavand men
reach here safely—"

She broke off and glided to the doorway. Fraser joined her
there, wondering at the brave soul within her which had revolted against the bloodshed, yet which had carried through
the plan unfalteringly—the soul which based all hopes on the
death of Al Hudr, yet which could not stoop to his assassination.

"Allah be good to you, Sefid!" he said softly, catching her
hand and drawing it to his lips. "You are a true daughter of
Tahir Beg—ah! I wonder if he is close enough to see this fire
and to take advantage of it!"

As Sefid turned to him in surprise, he swiftly related the
news borne by Winkler. Even now, it might be, Tahir Beg and
his riders were waiting to drop out of the hills upon the doomed
city of the Shaitan parasts!

"It may be, it may be!" exclaimed Sefid, excitement blazing in her face. "Remember, my father is an Aorami—he knows these mountains and all the folk in them, and the hidden trails! If Al Hudr is slain, then the Yezidis will obey me—"

"Obey you?" questioned Fraser.

"Yes—because the brazen peacock is their god, and is here with me! Al Hudr would guess that I had a hand in the plot, yonder; the Yezidis would think otherwise—did I not tell them that I had come to give them warning? They are so full of superstition that if Al Hudr is dead I can make them believe anything I say. But he has many secret ways about the palace, and I am afraid that he will escape—"

Fraser glanced about the tower chamber. A ladder ran to the room above and to the roof; the stone walls were solid, without a break—yet he remembered what Sefid had said about the secret passages.

"If there are hidden ways of reaching here," he reflected, "Al Hudr will use them to overpower us—"

"Certainly," was her calm response. "But we must hold the room above, and the roof, which is built for defense! The whole hope of my plot was that Al Hudr might be killed and that I might then, occupying this place, bend the foolish Yezidis to my wishes. Now that the Jaf men and the Hamavands are coming, now that Tahir Beg is somewhere near, we must hold the place until they arrive. Al Hudr will not want to harm me, therefore he may wait to starve us out. We shall see!"

Curiously enough, thought Fraser, she spoke as though convinced that the Persian would escape from the deathtrap, yonder!

BY THIS time the fire in the outer city had broadened to a deep glare that lighted the walls and the sky redly. Within the gardens was a closer and more awful conflagration; the wooden palace, alight as though fired in a dozen places, was shooting upward in blazing fury. Amid the crackling roar of the flames all lesser sounds were lost; only here and again came a shot, or some thin, keen yell of "Allah!" to tell of strife.

The men of Sulaimanieh could not, of course, hope for more than to die like warriors, sword in hand. To effect more than a mad slaughter of the infidels, was not their aim; they could not escape, nor did they want to escape. The wild fanaticism of the *muslim,* the "enlightened," had seized upon them, and they were running amuck like rabid dogs, hoping to atone for their own past and to win Paradise by dying greatly.

"I must go out and be ready to guide them through the pools, if any escape and reach here," said Sefid quietly. "No, do not come; remain here, both of you, and have your rifles ready! You may serve better by staying here to cover my return."

Out across the maze of shallow pools whose water glinted scarlet, she passed, her slender white figure gleaming eerily in the mounting light of the fire that was now slavering its red tongue over all things and bringing day into the black night. On the far side of the water she paused and stood there in the open, waiting; none who arrived from the palace could fail to see her. Fraser clenched his hands at thought of her danger, as he stood there motionless, searching the empty gardens for any sign of peril to her. Then he felt Winkler touch his arm, and he turned.

"Upon my word, sir, she's marvelous!" Winkler was staring wide-eyed after the girl. "Just the mere beauty of her, Mr. Robert—it shines through her, like a flame inside—and just as cool as you and I are! I don't know when I've seen so remarkable a young woman, sir—"

"Thank you, Winkler," and Fraser chuckled as he clapped the other on the back. "I knew you'd come around to my viewpoint when you'd met her."

Winkler gave him a startled look, choked back a sudden comprehending expostulation, and then slowly smiled.

"Yes, sir; I congratulate you very heartily, Mr. Robert. I only hope," he added slyly, "that your father does also."

"I hope he does—for his own sake," said Fraser. "Ah! There's someone coming—see here, suppose you get up to the roof of this place! Take a couple of extra rifles and be ready to use 'em if I shout."

Winkler vanished inside the tower.

The palace had now become a roaring pinnacle of fire; the whole building must have caught like a vast torch, for every corner of it seemed in flames, soaring in a great burst of almost smokeless scarlet light, transforming the whole sky into crimson. Bright as day were the gardens under this terrible light, and Fraser had discerned a running figure that approached the tower. He saw Sefid watching the figure also, her hands upraised to shield her face from the fierce heat of the conflagration.

Then he saw her beckon to the man, turn, and start toward the tower. He lowered his rifle, recognizing one of the two Hamavands.

"It was kind of Al Hudr to provide this neat little place for us," he reflected. "Attackers could get through these pools, of course, but they would be delayed—and we could decimate them in the attempt! The tower itself hasn't an opening that I've seen; the door would have to be battered away or a hole blown through the walls—and Al Hudr is not going to take any chances on killing Sefid. Well, here's one of our friends; no more are in sight, poor devils! The Sulaimanians certainly served us well tonight—Shaik Nuri showed them how to die, and they learned the lesson."

SEFID REACHED him, and behind her stumbled the Hamavand, who greeted Fraser with a hoarse cry of wild exultation and halted.

"Greeting, brother! Praise be to Allah, we have struck the infidel a blow this night. However, Al Hudr has escaped; I think his armor saved him. How the man fought! Idolater or not, he is a lion—"

"You're alone?" demanded Fraser. "Did none of the others escape—"

"None, so far as I know," returned the Hamavand coolly. "My comrade was slain, and the Yezidis are running down the men of Sulaimanieh like wolves." A laugh broke harshly from him. "Al Hudr, may his grave be desecrated, is still seeking Sefid in the bonfire yonder; but he will be searching the gardens soon enough. A rifle for me? Good!"

The mountaineer was unhurt, by a miracle.

"True enough," said Sefid. "They will be searching the gardens. Let us wait a moment or two more—if none of the Sulaimanians come, we can go into the tower and shut the door."

They waited; a nervous, tense time wherein the minutes dragged into hours. The palace fire was at its height—a vast crackling uproar of flames, so close that the heat was blistering.

Then, suddenly, they perceived on either hand hordes of running figures. A startled yell from Winkler, up above, reached them in warning. Yezidis these, enemies all!

"In!" cried Sefid. "Close the door—thrust out upon the bar and it closes itself!"

Fraser, who had given his rifle to the Hamavand, watched them enter, then bent above the iron bar that propped the door ajar. It was hot to the touch, so hot that he recoiled with a startled exclamation; but, spurred by a rifle-shot and the whine of a bullet flying from the stones of the tower, he gripped the bar of iron and threw his weight on it. For a space it did not move. The door, a great slab of iron seven feet by four hung at an angle, responded no whit to his effort.

"The bar! Throw it outward!" came the voice of Sefid.

Fraser gathered himself desperately, flung his weight against the iron bar with a savage intensity. This time it gave—unexpectedly. Carried off his balance by the sudden give, he staggered for an instant, and that instant was fatal. The pivoted door swung down and in; Fraser tried to spring backward, and failed. The great slab of iron struck him glancingly and hurled him, stunned, a dozen feet away. Fraser heard the harsh, reverberant clang as it clashed shut—then all the flaming sky went black for him.

PARTIES OF the Yezidis came dashing forward, having seen the figure of Sefid and knowing that here was the woman they had been sent to find. As they closed in about the tower, however, they were suddenly halted by the shallow pools of water, among which they slipped and stumbled in panic, fearing some unknown trap.

And, stumbling thus, bullets began to drive among them. Two rifles spoke from the roof of the tower—two riflemen shooting as fast as they could use the loaded weapons that lay ready to their hands. With shouts of dismay the attackers broke, gave way, plunged back to shelter. Before their eyes that tower had suddenly closed tightly, and they suspected magic in it.

They ran to the edge of the clearing, then formed in groups. Suddenly amazement and fear seized upon them, at sight of a white figure which appeared on the parapet of the tower, standing erect before them and upholding in her hands the brazen peacock! In that brilliant firelight every detail stood out plainly; words could not be heard for the roaring of the flames, but none were needed. She stood thus for a moment, then vanished.

The Yezidis paused, irresolute, their ranks constantly swelled by new arrivals. They dared not attack, because of the bullets which had strewn their dead among the shallow pools of water, and because Al Hudr had issued stern orders that Sefid be unharmed. While they stood thus hesitant, before their eyes the great iron door of the tower slowly swung open; it was swung outward by two men, and in the opening they saw Sefid, still bearing that brazen peacock. The woman, no less than the sacred image, struck awe into them.

Then, before them all, Sefid suddenly ran forth, stooped above the figure of Fraser, and pulled him back to safety. The two men with her held open the door, obviously with tremendous effort; Sefid had rejoined them before a man of the enemy could move, and as she vanished, dragging Fraser behind her, the door came shut again with a clang. To those who looked on in awe, the tower stood bare and unapproachable. Al Hudr had been sent for, but he came not. Instead, came orders from him bidding the Yezidis remain where they were and to attempt no attack.

So, fearing him, they remained at the edge of the clearing about the tower, and waited. The great blast of the conflagration was over; the palace was reduced to flaming pinnacles; dying grandeur, amid which its ancient stone portions remained incandescent, white-hot. Yet there was no lack of light. An area of the outer city was still blazing, and many of the Yezidis now withdrew outside the palace grounds; from the outer city, too, was rising a great clamor and a strident shouting, punctuated by rattling shots, so that it seemed some riot had burst forth. More and more of the crowd about the tower slipped away.

Upon regaining the shelter of the tower in safety—no little to their surprise—Winkler and the Hamavand were ordered to the roof by Sefid.

"Up with you!" she cried impatiently, standing above the senseless figure of Bob Fraser. "I can attend to him—you must be on the roof lest they try to scale the walls!"

"There is sense to that," growled the Hamavand, and Winkler reluctantly abandoned Fraser to the care of Sefid, and ascended with the Kurd to the roof to await developments.

THE RIFLES reloaded, they crouched behind the parapet and awaited the attack—which did not materialize. Not a Yezidi stirred to approach the tower, not a shot was directed toward the two defenders; the dark groups clustering about the edge of the garden clearing seemed to be awaiting some event in silence.

"Sheep without a leader!" spat the Hamavand expressively. "Wait till Al Hudr comes!"

Waiting was nervous work, however, and the chieftain did not appear. Gradually the two men realized that instead of the groups about the tower being augmented, they were rapidly lessening in numbers. Nor was the cause far to seek.

"There is fighting in the city," observed the Kurd, listening, "and the fire-glare is widening. Those Sulaimanians must not be all dead yet—hark to the shots!—and doubtless Al Hudr is there. Ask the lady Sefid to come up here, brother."

Winkler went to the ladder top and called Sefid. Obtaining no answer, he descended through the upper room to the lower chamber; he stood there at the foot of the ladder, staring around in petrified astonishment. Bob Fraser and Sefid had vanished bodily!

The great iron door was closed. Winkler had been watching from the roof, and knew that they had not left the tower. Yet— they were not here! He called frantically, and obtained no answer. The Hamavand above, hearing his voice and conjecturing that something was wrong, came down the ladder—and stood staring blankly. Then a sudden furious oath burst from him.

"Al Hudr—may he roast in hell!—slipped in here by some secret passage and carried them both away—see! Here is proof, by Allah!"

Stooping, the Kurd picked up a torn white scrap—a bit of Sefid's dress. But Winkler stared at the blank stones around him, utter despair in his eyes; and in his heart he echoed the blazing imprecations of his comrade.

CHAPTER XVI

BOB FRASER wakened to a sense of suffocation, which proceeded from cloths wound about his head. He found that he was bound hand and foot; also, he presently realized that he was being carried—he could feel hands upon him, and could hear the grunting of those who bore him. He lay quiet, and tried to think out what had happened.

His last memory was of the iron door knocking him sprawling. It abode with him sharply, for his head was dizzy and ached abominably. Knowing nothing of his rescue, he concluded that he had been carried off a prisoner by the Yezidis. A moment later he was confirmed in this belief by hearing the voice of Al Hudr, which he recognized instantly.

"Set down the Nazarene and see if he is dead. Give me a cup of wine—the White Pearl has fainted. Drink if you will, brethren; there is no further need for silence. How many of those fools were on the roof of the tower, I know not—let them stay there until they starve!"

Upon hearing the name of Sefid, Fraser started with sudden fear. Then he felt himself dropped on the earth, and the cloth was jerked away from about his head. He did not open his eyes, however, but lay motionless.

"He is not dead, lord," said a Kurdish voice, "but he is sense-less."

"Then disturb him not," answered Al Hudr with a short laugh. "Let him sleep until he is crucified, the infidel dog! Two of you go back outside and bring down here four eunuchs from the harem building, which has escaped the fire. Know you where the opening lies?"

"No, lord," answered a voice. "We have never known its secret, until tonight, and you summoned us in such haste that we took small note of the way—"

"Very well," snapped the chieftain impatiently. "Go back the way we came, and the opening will bring you out to the left of the shrine, among the trees. Note well the entrance and bring back the eunuchs at once. Here is my ring, to be your author-ity."

Fraser opened his eyes cautiously, and by degrees became aware of what place he was in; some underground chamber, he had guessed from the talk. So Sefid was here! What had hap-pened at the tower, he could only conjecture.

He found himself lying on the ground, fast bound. Above and behind him, out of his range of vision, men were drinking and discussing the events of the night; he guessed, from the voices, that there were but two remaining, and they were of Al Hudr's mercenaries. A lamp was hanging overhead. Wine jars stood along the walls. Evidently, then, this was the wine-cellar of the palace, or some chamber along a secret passage that had been stored for Al Hudr's use.

TWENTY FEET distant, Fraser beheld the figure of Sefid lying on a divan, while above her stooped Al Hudr, a wine-cup in his hand. The chieftain was attempting to revive the girl, and an instant later the attempt was more successful than he had thought, evidently.

Without warning, Sefid's hand flashed a knife from her bosom and struck. An exclamation broke from Al Hudr, then he had caught her hand and was laughing.

"So, White Pearl!" he mocked her gently. "This is the measure of your love for me, eh?"

He twisted the knife from her hand and tossed it into a corner. Sefid sat up, then rose.

"Love?" she repeated scathingly. "Think not that you will ever have love from me, idolater!"

"Others have said the same, but have changed their minds," and Al Hudr laughed. Admiration gleamed in his stern eyes as he watched her. "What a woman you are, White Pearl! Did you think that I would hold anger against you for this night's work? Nay! It was a shrewd blow, but no great harm is done. A palace is destroyed—another can be rebuilt! Those traitors of Sulaim- anieh slew a few of my men—and by this time they are dead, save for those who held the tower with you. And I can kill them if I so desire, or starve them.

"Your rescue of this Nazarene was a bold deed, Sefid, and I love you for it! Aye, I was watching from the secret passage, and I saw you pull into the tower as your men held open the door. A brave deed—although it might have ended otherwise had I not ordered my men to do you no hurt! And now it is all over, Sefid; the Sulaimanians are dead, the fires are being quenched, you are in hand again, and ere dawn the Nazarene shall be gasping on a cross at the gates. And with me is Melek Taus—"

As he spoke, Al Hudr gestured toward the brazen peacock, which he had brought from the tower and had set upon a wine-jar close at hand.

"Agha Fraser fooled me well," he continued, his face darken- ing. "I thought that he was getting the image from Tahir Beg— and all the while, you had it! Well, it was a clever game, but I am the winner of it; and the Nazarene shall be nailed to beams in payment. Thanks be to Azazil that there was no wind this night, else had all the inner buildings gone up in flames! "

"Would that they had," retorted Sefid bitterly, "and you with them!"

Al Hudr smiled. Then, as he saw the girl's eyes leap to Bob Fraser, he wheeled suddenly and realized that the American was awake. The conversation had made clear to Fraser what had taken place, and he knew that there was now no mercy to be expected.

"It's too bad you came through the affray unhurt, Al Hudr," he said. "You're more of a fool than I thought you were—a fool for luck, goes the proverb."

The chieftain snarled at him.

"We shall see how bravely you are talking after sunrise, Nazarene—a few hours of hanging on the nails lays bare the soul of a man! But where are those accursed eunuchs? Go out into the passage, one of you, and call."

One of the two Kurds swaggered past Al Hudr to a curtained entrance, passed into a dark passage beyond, and shouted. He returned, shaking his head.

"I heard no answer, lord—and the way is dark."

"Hell swallow the fools!" snapped Al Hudr.

FOR A moment he stood in frowning thought, then strode to Sefid in sudden decision and grasped her wrists. She fought against him, but vainly.

"Come hither and tie her arms!" Al Hudr commanded the grinning men. They obeyed, and Sefid stood raging but helpless. "I will go ahead, with her; do you carry the Nazarene and follow. There is work to be done up above, and I have no time to be lingering here in talk. Those black devils shall shriek under whips tomorrow!"

Thus swore Al Hudr, not knowing that his two messengers had been slain, and the eunuchs with them, and that the sword had entered into Penjivan, the unconquered!

Thrusting the brazen peacock beneath his waistcloth, Al Hudr took in one hand the bound wrists of Sefid, and in the other the hanging lamp; he urged the girl forward, and the two Kurds quickly picked up Fraser and followed. Then one of them, grumbling, got out his knife and slashed at the bonds around Fraser's ankles.

"Are we camels, to carry this infidel," growled the man. "Let him walk—and hold a knife to his back, brother!"

To all this Al Hudr made no objection, but led the way along a narrow passage that was plainly a relic of ancient times, for it was floored and walled with hewn stones. Sefid, knowing that all resistance was futile, offered none, but walked along as proudly as though she had won her bold game, instead of having lost it utterly—and herself with it! Fraser, his wrists still bound, was helpless in the grip of his two guards.

The passageway seemed to wind and twist interminably; nor, indeed, was it any short distance that the tunnel covered. When at last Al Hudr came to a halt, Fraser saw that before the party was a door of heavy beams. This Al Hudr swung open. Beyond appeared stone steps leading upward, and in the light of the lamp that the chieftain carried, a trap door appeared overhead.

Al Hudr paused, and summoned one of the Kurds to lift this door. The man pushed past and applied his weight; the door swung upward and fell away.

The party left the secret passage behind, and Fraser saw that they had emerged in a corner of the gardens, cloaked with trees, between the harem buildings and the shrine of the Yezidis. From Al Hudr came a startled word, as he pressed forward.

"What is this—there is fighting in the city! Are those Sulaimanians not yet dead?"

Fighting there was, indeed, as the babel of shouts and clamorings and shots bore full witness. The blazing pyre of the palace had burned itself nearly out, yet there was a broad glare of fire across the sky, and with visible haste and uneasiness Al Hudr led his party from among the trees, dashing down the lamp as he went.

They emerged suddenly in a wide area of light—they had come out upon the opening before the shrine. And here, in blank amazement, all paused.

The inner city seemed filled with confusion; on all sides rifles were spitting, men were running and fighting and slaying, and above the uproar rang out wild yells of "Allahu!" Al Hudr and his two men were stricken aghast by the spectacle, for the night was turned into day by the glare from the burning city. Fraser, however, awoke to mad realization of what it all meant.

"Take this dog to the gates and crucify him!" snapped Al Hudr. "This—"

"Tahir Beg!" The shout broke from Fraser and lifted through the din. "Tahir Beg! To the rescue, Hamavands! Tahir Beg!"

CURSING, ONE of the guards smote Fraser across the mouth; he reeled, laughing under the blow—laughing in wild exultation. Al Hudr loosed his hold on Sefid and sprang away— too late did he realize the truth, too late did he comprehend the dread fate that had come upon him and his city!

Before Al Hudr could take two steps, a wild mob of men was surging down upon the party. The two mercenaries clutched at the rifles slung over their shoulders—they were caught in the swirling mob and went down to death. All about him Fraser saw the fierce faces of Jafs and Hamavands; fighting to reach Sefid, he glimpsed Al Hudr, scimitar in hand, clearing a little space around him. The chieftain had become a madman, frothing at the lips, insensate under this blow of fate that had stricken him so terribly!

And then, suddenly, a roar sounded above the shouts and clamor, and the crowd fell back from Al Hudr. Through their ranks leaped Tahir Beg, revolver in hand; with but a glance toward Sefid and Fraser, who now stood together, the great Kurd planted himself before Al Hudr.

"Ho, Idolater!" he bellowed furiously. "Ho, ravisher of maidens, mocker of hospitality! Pray now to your false god!"

Al Hudr, who was unarmed except for that terrible sword of his, cast one quick glance around and saw that there was no escape. He drew himself erect, with a proud gesture.

"Shoot, then," he said simply.

Tahir Beg hurled the revolver away, with a great laugh of delight.

"By the right of the lord of the faithful, I am no butcher!" he swore. "Give me a blade like his, some of you—hasten! Did I not say that some day I would measure weapons with you, Persian? Well, I am here!"

Already Fraser and Sefid had been freed of their bonds by the Hamavands who pressed about them. Tahir Beg, bareheaded, took the curved blade that one of his men passed into his hand, and shook it at Al Hudr joyfully. The Persian had lost his green mantle, and his helmet with it; he was clad only in his chain-mail that enveloped his body to the knees.

"Room!" shouted Tahir Beg. "Room, in the name of Allah! Now, Persian, let us see whether God or Shaitan be stronger—"

"Azazil!" yelled Al Hudr, and leaped to the attack.

The watching circle of men fell silent. With every moment others were joining the crowd, and these also became silent as they watched the two figures in the center; Fraser, with Sefid's hands in his, felt her fingers clench convulsively.

AL HUDR was upon the great Kurd like a falcon—striking, evading, darting in and out with the swiftness of light; no less agile was Tahir Beg, and no less master of his weapon. They had come up, these twain, from the old days when swords ruled the hills and rifles were rare in the land, and with them they had brought a skill with the blade that few men could match today.

Before them, between them, over them, the scimetars whirled like scarlet brands in the light of the conflagration. Steel struck on steel, sparks glimmered from the meeting of the blades, blow followed blow with the rapidity of light; yet the two were untouched. Each of them a fighting man by birth, by divine grace, they fought not alone with muscles and brute strength, but with the sixth sense that only such men possess.

Upon the swelling crowd abode a deathlike silence. Above them, unheeded, floated the canopy of flames from the outer

city, the clamor and shots and uproar. Here was only a dread
stillness, through which sounded the hoarse breathing of the
fighters, the stamping of their feet on the stone flags, the clash
and ring of the scimetars. With Tahir Beg was the fierce craving
for vengeance; with Al Hudr, the utter ferocity of the trapped
animal. Death hovered above them visibly in the reeking skies.
No voice was raised to urge Tahir Beg onward, and none was
needed; yet, in the silence, Al Hudr could not but feel the
enmity that ringed him in, the deep hatred gleaming from every
eye. He was cooler now, his frothing rage mastered, and he
fought venomously.

Like lightning were his blows, but Tahir Beg laughed as his
blade circled and parried them, and swung hissing back at Al
Hudr. Then, suddenly, the Kurd staggered and reeled backward;
from all the crowd broke a low gasping breath, and Al Hudr
sprang forward to cut terribly—but the cut was parried. Tahir
Beg lifted his left hand and wiped a red smear from his eyes as
it trickled downward.

"Allahu!" he croaked, and plunged at the chieftain.

Now a new figure pushed forward amid the crowd—a tall,
broad-shouldered figure. Bob Fraser did not see it, for his gaze
was riveted to the fighters; but Al Hudr saw it, saw the grim,
implacable countenance of Howard Z. Frazer there looking on
silently, and his teeth bared in a dreadful snarl.

"You next—after—this jackal!" he cried hoarsely. Few knew
to whom he referred, for no eye was lifted from the battle to
seek new arrivals, but Tahir Beg guessed aright, and laughed
hoarsely.

"The jackal bites!" he uttered, and his blade rang against the
chain-mail of Al Hudr—reached it for the first time, although
it slid harmlessly from the mail. He struck again with terrible
strength. Al Hudr countered the blow, but with a clash and
clang his jeweled scimetar flew shattered into gleaming shreds
of steel.

Tahir Beg checked himself, drew back swiftly.

"Give the dog another weapon!"

Al Hudr, standing empty-handed, spat a curse and seized the nearest weapon of those extended to him. Again he rushed at the Kurd, again the blades curved and glimmered and bit in the red glare.

From the crowd leaped forth a gasping cry—blood sprang suddenly to the chainmail of Al Hudr, a thin trickle of red where Tahir Beg's point had ripped. But it was no mortal hurt, and the sting of it redoubled the furious energy of the chieftain.

THEY WERE wearying now, wearying fast both of them. Sweat dripped from their faces, and again Tahir Beg wiped the crimson smear from his brow. Their breath came from clenched teeth, sharp and hoarse and panting. No longer could the crowd bear that frightful tensity in silence; cries began to rise from all sides in wild incoherence: "Allah upon him!" "May Shaitan seize his feet!" "Strike, in the name of God!" "Weaken, infidel, weaken!"

The blows became more furious as both men felt the strain. Al Hudr's point ripped at the shoulder of Tahir, but at this the great Kurd plunged forward madly, ferociously. His scimitar whined down and again down in a tempest of clashing strokes, nor could Al Hudr altogether meet that storm with his whirling steel. He began to give ground, he began to dodge, he began to shrink from the onslaught. The end was not far.

Al Hudr slipped. He fell forward and came to his knees, and, knowing that he could not rise in time, he remained thus, his hands flung out before him, the breath bursting from his lungs in great gasps. It seemed that in his raging shame of defeat he could not face his enemies again, but Tahir Beg, withholding his arm, spat at him in scorn.

"Up, idolater! Up, and pray to your false god!"

Finding that there was no stroke to bring death so easily, Al Hudr rose. Now upon him burst the Kurd with a hurricane of clanging strokes, pressing him backward, driving him among the circle of men who gave ground in wild confusion. To this side and that roved the desperate, hollow eyes of Al Hudr, and found no escape. He struck at his enemy again, desperately, gathered all his strength and struck in a terrible effort to break through the gleaming circle of steel and find the life of the Kurd.

His blows failed—and as they failed, as the arm of Al Hudr drooped in an instant of desperate weariness, Tahir Beg flashed down his scimetar. Al Hudr tried to meet that lightning sweep, but his blade was dashed away; the steel drove at his neck above the edge of the chain-mail, drove down and bit deep into his breast. He threw out his arms and reeled backward.

"Allah!" gasped Tahir Beg. He stood as though dazed, his eyes fiercely alight, his nostrils quivering with great breaths. Then, as the crowd began to surge forward, he lifted his weapon above the dead body of Al Hudr, and wiped the blood from it with his sleeve.

"The fate of every man is written in his forehead," he exclaimed. "Praise be to Allah!"

Bob Fraser drew a deep breath—and turned to meet the eyes of his father.

CHAPTER XVII

FINIS CORONAT OPUS

T HE DOWNTOWN offices which housed the many
and varied financial activities of Howard Z. Fraser, looked
forward to his return with a unanimous lack of joy. The morning
newspapers had carried a brief account of the arrival of his yacht
in quarantine, and the officers knew that he could be expected
to descend upon them at any minute.

Nor could the underlings who acknowledged his sway of
iron be greatly blamed for this joyless prospect. During the past
three years their master had become known among them as
"The Boss Grouch"; and their freedom from his attention in
the past few months had been as a glorious vacation to all who
served him.

"Gee, ain't it fierce?" mourned the office boy. "He'll stomp in
an' growl somethin' under his breath, and stomp on into his own
office—an' there'll be hell to pay all down the line! It'll be just
like he hadn't been away more'n a day!"

Thus, when a stenographer from one of the front offices
spread the information that his well-known limousine was
drawing up in the street outside, something like a groan ascended from everyone. The noon hour had just concluded.

When Howard Z. Fraser crossed the threshold of his offices
and paused there, however, his appearance was hailed with a
general gasp of amazement; every eye was fastened upon him
in unconcealed wonder. Here was not the man they had
known—here was a new man! Here was a man ten years

younger, whose eye sparkled with vitality and the joy of life—a man come home again as though he had found the Fountain of Youth!

"Hello, everybody!" shouted Howard Z. Fraser with a joyous lack of dignity. "How's everything? Where's Smithers?"

Smithers, the general manager, came rushing forward through astounded ranks. The Boss Grouch seized his hand and shook it vigorously, beamingly.

"Well, well, if it isn't great to be back!"

Fraser shook hands delightedly with everyone, and when Smithers nervously mentioned certain affairs of business, Fraser positively brushed him aside.

"Business? Nothing doing today, Smithers—nothing today! I have more important affairs on hand. I came down to get that jewel case out of my safe; get it for me, will you, old man?"

SMITHERS STAGGERED off to get the jewel case that had reposed for years in the private safe in the inner office. Fraser continued his hand-shaking, beaming with delight and showering cordiality on every hand.

The Fraser mansion, meantime, was being hurriedly turned inside out by a frantic corps of servants under directions from Winkler, who was the only cool and self-possessed person on the premises. At three-thirty a car delivered a somewhat flustered clerical gentleman, who was promptly ushered into the private library of Howard Z. Fraser; after ushering in the clergyman, Winkler closed the door and stood at attention.

"Here, Doctor—you remember Bob?" exclaimed Fraser. "Sefid, allow me to present the Reverend Doctor Jones—we decided at the last minute, Doctor, to have a private ceremony here in this room, for personal reasons. Hope we haven't rushed you—and this is my old friend Gholam Ali Tahir Beg Aorami—he isn't a Christian, Doctor, although Miss de Montfort has decided to embrace that faith—"

"God bless my soul!" murmured the dazed cleric, staring from the blushing, happy face of Sefid to the laughing Bob

Fraser, and from the exuberant Howard Z. Fraser to the hugely mustached features of Tahir Beg. The great Kurd was clad in frock-coat and all the accompaniment thereof; the garments were not comfortable to him, but being a gentleman he wore them with a grand air.

"We'll have it all over by four," hastened on Howard Z. Fraser, "and then we'll hold the reception, and—Winkler! You and Tahir Beg are to be the witnesses, so stand out! All ready, Doctor."

The reverend gentleman found his prayer-book thrust into his hand by Bob Fraser, and then stood motionless for a moment. At length he directed his gaze downward, with a perceptible sniffing. Beneath his feet was the ancient and incredible dirty Kurdish rug.

"Don't mind it," and Howard Z. Fraser clapped him on the shoulder. "It's a good smell when you get used to it, Doctor—why, Tahir Beg will sit there all day long and dream that he's back in Kurdistan!"

WITH A helpless look around, Doctor Jones, probably feeling that this general levity was most indecorous and out of place, opened his book and proceeded to earn the fat fee that was in readiness for him. He was to receive another shock when Tahir Beg affixed his signature as witness in flowing Persian characters.

At four o'clock most of the guests had assembled and with them newspaper men from every sheet in the city—admitted by express invitation of the host. Flowers decked the great rooms, buffets groaned beneath the weight of caterers' delicacies, and more than one jaded business man brightened visibly when ice-frosted buckets of silver became visible, and it proved evident that prohibition had not affected the Fraser cellars.

The door of the private library opened, and Howard Z. Frazer promptly introduced his son and daughter to his assembled guests *en masse*. Then, leaving Bob to do the explaining, he rushed away on an important errand.

The nature of this errand was made clear when Winkler opened the dining room doors and exposed to view the table bearing a huge bride-cake. Beside it stood Howard Z. Fraser, who lifted his hand for attention and then indicated the cake.

"Here, my friends," he exclaimed, "is a slight surprise for the bride and groom—this object which you see adorning the cake is a historic symbol which is supposed to represent a peacock. It has been vitally connected with certain experiences we have had in Kurdistan, and it has brought the best luck in the world to me and to my son. Sefid, my dear! Come here and cut the cake—and make the brazen peacock bring you the best of luck in years to come!"

Howard Z. Fraser admitted afterward that he had intended to tell exactly what the brazen peacock was—but upon meeting the eye of the Reverend Doctor Jones his nerve had failed him. However, the clerical gentleman read all about the image of Melek Taus in the next morning's papers; and if he was shocked, he said nothing of it.

H . BEDFORD-JONES

BEDFORD-JONES IS a Canadian by birth, but not by profession, having removed to the United States at the age of one year. For over twenty years he has been more or less profitably engaged in writing and traveling. As he has seldom resided in one place longer than a year or so and is a person of retiring habits, he is somewhat a man of mystery; more than once he has suffered from unscrupulous gentlemen who impersonated him—one of whom murdered a wife and was subsequently shot by the police, luckily after losing his alias.

The real Bedford-Jones is an elderly man, whose gray hair and precise attire give him rather the appearance of a retired foreign diplomat. His hobby is stamp collecting, and his collection of Japan is said to be one of the finest in existence. At present writing he is en route to Morocco, and when this appears in print he will probably be somewhere on the Mojave Desert in company with Erle Stanley Gardner.

Questioned as to the main facts in his life, he declared there was only one main fact, but it was not for publication; that his life had been uneventful except for numerous financial losses, and that his only adventures lay in evading adventurers. In his younger years he was something of an athlete, but the encroachments of age preclude any active pursuits except that of motoring. He is usually to be found poring over his stamps, working at his typewriter, or laboring in his California rose garden, which is one of the sights of Cathedral Cañon, near Palm Springs.

Bedford-Jones has written stories laid in many corners of the earth, but among his most popular tales were the John Solomon stories which started many years ago in the *Argosy*.